A playful and provocative Regency trilogy from
CHRISTINE MERRILL

Ladies in Disgrace

In London's High Society, there are three unconventional women who are not afraid to break the rules of social etiquette! And it will take a certain type of rake to tame these delectably disgraceful ladies…!

Look for

Lady Folbroke's Delicious Deception
March 2012

Lady Drusilla's Road to Ruin
April 2012

Lady Priscilla's Shameful Secret
May 2012

D1022899

Author Note

I went into this story wondering why more people didn't have blind heroes. By the time I was halfway through writing I knew.

It had seemed a simple enough thing at first. But after a few days of writing, I noticed how much of what we put into a book relies on the sense of sight. Removing the visual cues from my story made me learn to use my other senses to feel what my hero was feeling. And I needed to remember the dimensions of my imaginary rooms, just as he did, to navigate my way through them, one pace at a time.

And then there was the illusory idea that blind might not mean totally blind, and that there were situations where a little sight was almost as bad as no sight at all. My eye doctor told me that the type of blindness I had given my hero would make him lose all sense of color, even if he could still distinguish some light and shadow.

And after a little research I found that many of the great advances in dealing with the loss of sight were several years in the future for Adrian. There would be no Braille until 1821. And, though it would come as a result of the very war that Adrian had fought, it would be meant to help the French defeat the English. The majority of education available to him in his own country would be vocational in nature, and far beneath his station.

For a man of Adrian's temperament, who had expected to control his world and his destiny, the adjustment would have been difficult. If he learned to accept his condition, his first reactions to it would leave him with much to apologize for.

Fortunately for him, I gave him Emily, who is a very patient woman.

CHRISTINE MERRILL

Lady Folbroke's Delicious Deception

Harlequin®

TORONTO NEW YORK LONDON
AMSTERDAM PARIS SYDNEY HAMBURG
STOCKHOLM ATHENS TOKYO MILAN MADRID
PRAGUE WARSAW BUDAPEST AUCKLAND

Recycling programs
for this product may
not exist in your area.

ISBN-13: 978-0-373-29681-1

LADY FOLBROKE'S DELICIOUS DECEPTION

Copyright © 2011 by Christine Merrill

First North American Publication 2012

CHRISTINE MERRILL

lives on a farm in Wisconsin, U.S.A., with her husband, two sons and too many pets—all of whom would like her to get off the computer so they can check their email. She has worked by turns in theater costuming, where she was paid to play with period ballgowns, and as a librarian, where she spent the day surrounded by books. Writing historical romance combines her love of good stories and fancy dress with her ability to stare out of the window and make stuff up.

To Dr. Eugene Swanson and his helpful staff.
Thanks for taking care of my eyes.

Chapter One

W̲hile Emily Longesley could say with truth that she did not dislike many people, she had begun to suspect that she hated her husband's cousin Rupert. There was something in the way he looked at the manor when he visited that made her think he wished to measure it for furniture.

It was all the more annoying to know that he was entitled to his feelings of possessiveness. If she remained childless, the title fell to Rupert. And as the years had passed since her husband had abandoned her, Rupert's visits had grown more frequent, more intrusive, and he'd become more generally confident in the eventuality of his inheritance. Lately, he had taken to giving an annoying smirk as he'd asked after the health of her husband, as though he were privy to some bit of information that she was not.

It was even more bothersome to suspect that this

might be the truth. Although her husband's secretary, Hendricks, insisted that the earl was well, he was equally insistent that Adrian had no desire to communicate with her. A visit from him was unlikely. A visit *to* him would be both unwelcome and out of the question. Were they hiding something, or was her husband's dislike of her as transparent as it appeared?

Today, she could stand it no longer. 'Rupert, what is the meaning of that expression on your face? It almost appears that you doubt my word. If you suspect that Adrian is ill, then the least you could do is pretend to be sympathetic.'

Rupert looked at her with a smug grin that seemed to imply he'd caught her at last. 'I do not suspect Folbroke of illness so much as I begin to doubt his existence.'

'What utter fustian. You know perfectly well that he exists, Rupert. You have known him since childhood. You attended our wedding.'

'And that was almost three years ago.' He glanced around him, as though the empty air were some recent discovery. 'I do not see him here, now.'

'Because he resides in London for most of the year.' All of the year, in fact, but it would not help to bring that to the fore.

'None of his friends has seen him there. When Parliament is in session, his seat in the House of Lords is vacant. He does not attend parties or the theatre. And when I visit his rooms, he is just gone out and not expected back.'

'Perhaps he does not wish to see you,' Emily said. If

so, she had found one point of agreement with her absent spouse.

'I do not particularly wish to see him, either,' Rupert said. 'But for the sake of the succession, I demand to see some evidence that the man still breathes.'

'That he still breathes? Of all the ridiculous things you have said, Rupert, I think that this is the worst. You are his closest living relative. And his heir. If the Earl of Folbroke had died, you would have been notified of it immediately.'

'If you chose to tell me.' He was looking at her with a suspicious cat's gaze, as though he was sure, if he stared long enough, she would admit to a body buried beneath the floorboards.

'Of course I would tell you if something had happened to Adrian. What reason would I have to conceal the truth from you?'

'Every reason in the world. Do you think I cannot see how you are left in charge of this property when he is absent? The servants take their orders from you. I have seen the steward and the man of business come to you for their instructions, and caught you poring over the account books as though you would have any idea what to do with them.'

After all the time she had spent reading them, she knew perfectly well what to do with the accounts. And her husband had no problem with her taking them on, even expressing his approval of her management in the few curt communications that had come to her through

Hendricks. 'Since you are not yet the earl, why should it matter to you?'

Rupert's eyes narrowed. 'Because it is unnatural. I do not wish to see my inheritance squandered through the mismanagement of a woman. I have written to Folbroke frequently with my fears. Yet there is no sign of him coming to take control of what is rightfully his. He is here so seldom that he might as well be dead. And perhaps he is, for all you seem to care. You have arranged the running of the place to your own satisfaction, have you not? But if he has passed and you think can maintain a charade that there is a master here, you are sorely mistaken.'

Emily gathered her breath, trying to remain calm in the face of the bombardment. Rupert had always been a bit of a pill, but she had done her best to be kind to him, for the sake of her husband. Her even temper had been wasted on both Adrian and his ridiculous cousin, and her patience had reached its end. 'Your accusations are ridiculous.'

'I think not, madam. The last time I visited his rooms, the servants claimed he was indisposed. But when I forced my way in to search for him, I could find no trace.'

'If you abuse his hospitality and bully his servants, then no wonder he does not wish to see you. Your behaviour is beyond rude. The fact that you have not seen him does not indicate that I have not. How do you think papers of business for this estate are signed? I cannot sign them myself.' Actually, she found her forgeries quite credible. And what could not be forged was passed through to her husband's secretary and then returned to her. Though she knew Hendricks to be as devoted to her husband as he was helpful to her. While there was no proof that these papers were forged as well, she sometimes had her suspicions.

But Rupert had no faith at all. 'On the contrary, I have no doubt that you could and do sign documents. Should a miracle occur, and I receive a letter from your husband, I will have no proof that his hand was the one that wrote it.'

'And I suppose you do not believe me when I say that I have contact with him regularly.'

Her cousin laughed. 'Of course I do not. I think it is a ruse to keep me from what is rightfully mine.'

His surety in the emptiness of her marriage had pushed her temper to the breaking point. 'This estate is not yours. None of it. It belongs to Adrian Longesley, the current Earl of Folbroke. And after him, to his son.'

Rupert laughed again. 'And when are we likely to see an heir from your invisible husband?'

The idea struck suddenly, and she could not help but express it. 'Quite possibly in eight months. Although it is just as likely to be a girl. But Adrian assures me that in his family the first child is almost always male.'

This seemed to deflate Rupert, who sputtered his next answer. 'You are…are…'

'Increasing. Yes.' Now that the first lie was out, it emboldened her to continue in it. 'I did not mean to be so unladylike to broach the subject of my condition, but since you insist on trying me with baseless suspicions, I have no choice. And I would think carefully, were I you, to speak what is probably in your mind and hint that it is not my husband's child at all. If I hear so much as a breath of that, I will tell Adrian how you speak to me when he is away. And he will think nothing of family connections and run you through for spreading salacious rumours about me. He was in the army, you know. He is still a crack shot, and a dab hand with a sword. And very sensitive of my feelings. He would not wish me to be hurt.' The last was the biggest lie of all. But what did it matter, next to her imaginary baby?

Rupert's face was white mottled with red, and his lips twitched as though she had pushed him so close to apoplexy that his speech had failed. Finally, he managed, 'If this is true, which I sincerely doubt it is, then I hardly know what to say of it.'

Emily smiled, turning his sly looks back upon him. 'Why, my dear cousin Rupert, that is simplicity itself. The only thing you must say to me is "Congratulations." And then, "Farewell." Women in my condition tire easily. And, alas, I have no more strength to socialise with you.' She gripped him by the hand in a way that might appear fond were it not so forceful, and gave a forward tug, propelling him past her to the doorway of the salon and allowing his momentum to carry him out into the hall. When he was clear of the door, she shut it quickly behind him and leaned her shoulders against the panel, as though that were all it would take to block out any further visits.

It had been bad enough, at the beginning of the interview, when she had feared that she would have to produce her wayward husband. But now she would be expected to produce both him and an infant—and get Adrian to agree that he had fathered the child, whether he had, or not.

Or not. Now there was an interesting possibility. At the moment, she had no admirers to encourage in so passionate a way. And while she did not think herself unattractive, she suspected that there were some things that even the loyal Hendricks would not do in the name of maintaining the status quo.

But if Adrian had any interest in her continued fidelity, than he had best get himself home at least long enough to prove his good health, if not his virility. She had not heard a word from him in almost a year. Although the servants swore that they had seen him, they did it with the sort of worried expressions that told her something was seriously amiss. And they followed their avowals with equally worried assurances, similar to Hendricks's, that there was no need for her to go to London to see for herself. In fact, that would be the worst possible thing for her to do.

It was a woman, she suspected. They were trying to shield her from the fact that her husband had taken up permanent residence with someone else. He was willing to let his own wife and the chance at a family go hang for a mistress and a brood of bastards.

She tried to tell herself she was being both ridiculous and overly dramatic. Most men had arrangements of some kind or other, and wives who were content to ignore them. But as months had turned to years, and he paid no attention at all to her, it grew harder to pretend that she did not care.

And at the moment, her problems were concerned less with what he might have done, and more with what he had not. While it was difficult to be the object of such a total rejection, it became untenable when it damaged her ability to stay in her own home. In her three years of residence here, she had come to think of Folbroke Manor as rightfully hers. And if the fool she had married was declared dead because he could not be bothered to appear, she would have to yield it to that oaf, Rupert.

It would result in inconvenience and bother to all concerned.

Emily glanced at the desk in the corner, and thought of composing a sternly worded letter on the subject. But this matter was far too urgent and too personal to risk exposing it to another's eyes. If, as she expected, Hendricks read all of my lord's mail, she did not wish him to know that she had resorted to requesting sexual congress in writing.

And it would be even more embarrassing if the answer came in someone else's hand, or not at all. Or worse yet, in the negative.

All things considered, it would be far better to make a sudden appearance in London, camp out in Adrian's rooms, and await his return. Once the servants saw that she was in earnest, they would accede to her perfectly logical demand for an audience with her own husband.

When she saw him, she would tell him that either he must get her with child, or tell the odious Rupert that he still breathed so that the man would leave her alone.

Then they could go back about their business of leading separate lives. And he could pretend she didn't exist, just as he obviously wished to.

Chapter Two

For the first time in ages, Emily was in the same city as Adrian Longesley. Scant miles apart—possibly even less than that. Even now, he might be in residence behind the closed door, just in front of her.

Emily fought down the wave of terror that the prospect aroused in her, placing her palm flat against the rain-spattered window glass of the carriage, willing herself to feel as cool as it did. The nearness to Adrian was a palpable thing, like a tug on a string tied to something vital, deep inside her. Although she had felt it for most of her life, she had learned to ignore it. But it grew stronger as the carriage had reached the outskirts of London, an annoying tightness in her chest, as though she could not quite manage to catch a full breath.

With that lack of breath would come the weakening of her voice, the quiet tone and the tendency to squeak without warning. And, worst of all, it would be impossible to talk to him. When she tried to speak, she would stammer things out, repeating herself or pausing inappropriately in the middle of a thought, only to have the words rush out in a jumble. Even if she could manage to stay silent, there would be the blushing, and the inability to meet his gaze.

And since she was sure that he felt no answering pull on this magical bond between them, her behaviour would irritate him. He would think her an idiot, just as he had from the first moment they'd married. And he would dismiss her again, before she could explain herself.

When dealing with Adrian, she found it much easier to express herself with written communication. When she had the time to compose her thoughts, and the ability to toss any false starts and missteps into the fire, she had no troubles making her point.

And in that she was the very opposite of her husband. He had been clear enough, when he'd bothered to speak to her. But the few letters she'd received were terse, full of cross hatching, and in a hand so rough as to be practically illegible. She suspected it was drink that caused it. While easy to decipher, the latest ones came with a brief preamble, explaining that my lord was indisposed and had dictated the following to Hendricks.

She glanced at her reflection in the watery glass. She had improved with age. Her skin had cleared. Her hair was better dressed. Despite her rustication, she took care to outfit herself in the latest styles. While she had never been a pretty girl, she counted herself a handsome woman. Although she did not agree with it, it flattered her that the word *beauty* had been applied by others. She had also been assured that her company was charming, and her conversation intelligent.

But to the one man she'd always longed to impress, she could not manage to behave as anything other than David Eston's troublesome little sister. She was sure that it was only out of loyalty to his friend and family that Adrian had been willing to saddle himself with such a dull and graceless creature.

Before her, her own image dissolved as the coachman opened the door and put down the step for her, holding an umbrella over her head as he rushed her to the door, knocking for her.

The door opened and her husband's butler greeted her with an open mouth and a breathless, 'My Lady Folbroke.'

'No need to announce me, Abbott. If you can find someone to take my cloak, I will make myself comfortable in the salon.'

When no footman appeared to help her, she untied the neck and stepped forwards out of the garment, letting it drop from her shoulders.

Abbott reached forwards, hurrying to catch it before it struck the floor. 'Of course, my lady. But my Lord Folbroke—'

'Is not expecting me,' she finished for him.

At the end of the hallway, her husband's secretary appeared, took one look at her, and then glanced behind him as though he wished, like a rabbit meeting a fox, to dart back under cover.

'Hello, Hendricks.' She smiled in a way that was both warm and firm, and pushed past the butler, bearing down on him.

'Lady Folbroke.' Hendricks looked quietly horrified to see her and repeated, 'You were not expected.'

'Of course not, Hendricks. Had he expected me, my darling Adrian would have been shooting in Scotland. Or on the Continent. Anywhere but sharing London with me.' She tried a light laugh to show how unimportant it was to her, and failed dismally. She ignored the strange, sharp feeling in her stomach and the ache in her heart that came from knowing she was not really wanted.

The secretary had the courtesy to look shamed by it, but made no effort to deny what she had said.

'I suppose it is too much to hope that he is here at the moment.'

'No, my lady. He is out.'

'That is the same story you give to his cousin Rupert, who has been tormenting me endlessly on the subject of Adrian's whereabouts. I have had enough of it, Hendricks.' She stopped to breathe, for while her tone had sufficient volume, she did not want it creeping into shrillness. Then she continued. 'My husband must accept that, if he cannot deal with his heir, he will have to deal with me. It is unfair of him to avoid us both. And while I am quite willing to shoulder the responsibility of land, tenants, crops and several hundred-odd sheep while Adrian gallivants about the city, the added burden of Rupert is simply too much, Hendricks. It is the last straw to this camel.'

'I see, Lady Folbroke.' Hendricks had replaced his hunted look with an expression of neutral courtesy, as though he hoped that his silence would still her questions.

'My husband is still in the city?' She gave the man a critical look.

He squirmed and nodded.

She nodded in reply. 'And how long might it be until he returns here?'

The secretary gave a helpless shrug.

'Honesty, Hendricks. You know more than you are saying, I am sure. All I require of you is a simple answer. I intend to wait as long as is needed, in either case. But it would be nice to know if I should request a light meal, or send for my trunks and prepare for an extended stay.'

'I do not know, Lady Folbroke.' There was a kind of hopelessness in the statement that made her almost believe the man.

'Surely he must tell you his plans when he goes out.'

'When he bothers to make them,' the secretary said, revealing a bitterness that smacked of honesty. 'If he sets an agenda, he rarely keeps to it. Sometimes he is gone for hours. And other times days.'

'Then he must be letting rooms elsewhere.'

'This may be true. But I do not know where, for I have never visited them. And when he returns?' Hendricks shook his head, clearly worried.

'I suppose he is foxed.' She gave a disgusted sigh. It was no less than she feared about him, but the confirmation did nothing to improve her mood.

'If that were all. He is…' Hendricks struggled to find a phrase that would not give up a confidence. 'Not well. Unhealthy, my lady. I doubt he eats. Or sleeps. When he can bring himself to come home after one of these excursions, he collapses for days at a time. I fear he will do himself an injury through self-neglect.'

'His father was around the same age when he lost his life, was he not?'

'Yes, my lady. A riding accident.'

It was gently put, as was everything Hendricks said. The man was a master of understatement. But she remembered the circumstances quite well, for the severity of the last earl's injuries had been the talk of the neighbourhood. Adrian's father had been the worse for drink, and riding hell for leather through the woods, taking jumps that other men would not have risked while sane and sober. The fall had killed both man and horse in a way that was neither quick nor painless.

Her brother had said nothing of his friend's reaction when the accident had occurred. But she could remember clearly the solemn darkness of the young man on the neighbouring estate, and the way it had both frightened and intrigued her. 'Perhaps it preys upon his mind. And all the more reason that I should be here to put a stop to it.'

The secretary looked both doubtful and hopeful, as though he could not decide where his loyalty might lie.

'Summon the coachman who took him when he departed, so that we might learn his destination. If we can find his normal haunts, then I will search them until I find him.'

'You cannot,' Hendricks leaned forwards, and she knew the situation must be serious for the taciturn man was clearly alarmed.

'I mean to do it, all the same.'

The man stared into her eyes, as though to gauge the strength of her resolve. Then he sighed. 'I will accompany you.'

'That is hardly necessary.'

Hendricks squared his shoulders, doing his best to look formidable. 'I am sorry, Lady Folbroke, but I must insist. If you mean to continue on this unadvisable course of action, than I cannot leave you to do it alone.'

'And who gives you the right to question me?'

'Lord Folbroke himself. He has been quite clear to me in his instructions, with regards to you. I am to assist you in all things, trust your judgement and obey you as I would him. But first and foremost, he trusts me to keep you from harm.'

The sentiment brought her up short. After a year of silence on his part, it had never occurred to her that her husband thought of her at all. And certainly not for a sufficiently protracted time as to concern himself with her safety. 'He worries about me?'

'Of course, my lady. He asks after you each time I return from Derbyshire. Normally, I assure him there is no reason to be concerned. But in this case?' He shook his head.

Emily dismissed the momentary feeling of warmth

at the picture of Adrian asking about her. 'If my welfare is his foremost desire, perhaps he could have seen fit to share it with me. Or he could make an effort to stay out of low haunts himself. Then it would not be necessary for me to seek him in a place he did not want me to go.'

Hendricks was frowning at the twisted logic of her statement, trying to find a rebuttal, so she allowed him no more time. She turned to the butler. 'Abbott, have the carriage brought around. Mr Hendricks and I will be going out. We will be returning with Lord Folbroke.'

She glared at Hendricks. 'Whether he likes it or not.'

'You are sure this is the place?' The building before her gave every indication of being just what it was: a villainous hole that was well below the genteel debauchery she'd expected.

'Yes, my lady,' Hendricks said, with a grim smile. 'Of late, the servants bring him here. He finds his own way home.'

She sighed. There was a sign swinging above the battered door that appeared to be a woman of limited virtue, and even more limited clothing. 'What is it called, then?'

'The Whore's Left...' Hendricks coughed as though he could not bring himself to finish the name.

'Is it a brothel?' She peered out the window at the grimy glass panes in front of her, trying not to show the curiosity she felt.

'No, my lady. A public house.'

'I see.' It was nothing like the rather conservative inn

in their village. But things were very different in London, she was sure. 'Very well, then. Wait in the carriage.'

'I most certainly will not.' It was a moment before the secretary realised how completely he'd overstepped his bounds in his effort to protect her. Then he said more softly, 'I have been through doors like that one, and seen the clientele inside. It is a dangerous place for Lord Folbroke and even more so for a woman alone.'

'I do not mean to be there long enough to experience risk. If he is there, he will think the same as you, and though he might choose the place for his own entertainment, he will be forced to escort me out of it. But I do not mean to leave without him.' She set her chin in the way she did, to let the Derbyshire servants know that she was brooking no more nonsense, and saw the secretary weaken before her.

'If you find him, he might not be willing to go.' Again there was a delicate pause as he searched for a way around her orders. 'You might need my help.'

It was perfectly true. She had no reason to believe that her husband would listen to her entreaties, if he would not answer her correspondence. 'Would you remove him by force, if needed?'

Hendricks paused again. To take her side when in the presence of her husband would seem close to mutiny. He had been Adrian's aide-de-camp in the army, and had the fierce loyalty of a soldier to a superior officer to match his dedication to a friend and employer. But then he said, as though the confession was a thing he did not want to share, 'If the instruction came from you, and it was meant for his own good, I would do it. There are reasons for his aberrant behaviour, which you will understand soon enough. But if he is no longer able to act in his own best interests, then someone must do it for him.'

Emily touched Hendricks's shoulder to reassure him. 'Do not fear for your position. I promise you will come to no harm for doing what is right. But we must be agreed on this before we begin. I will ask him to come. And if he does not, you must help me remove him.'

'Very well.' He nodded. 'Let us do the thing quickly, now that we are decided. The situation cannot stand as it does much longer.'

They walked through the door together, Hendricks close at her shoulder. And Emily stepped back into him as she took in the room before her. The sound of drunkenness hit her first: laughing, fighting and ribald song. And then the smell—urine and vomit added to the smoke from a blocked chimney and burned meat to make the room even more unpleasant. She had expected to find Adrian in some normal gaming hell where the play was deep and the women were not ladies. Or perhaps a whorehouse where the play was of a different sort entirely. But she had assumed it would be the sort of place where lords went, when they sought to amuse themselves outside polite society.

There was no sign of even the lowest members of their set in evidence. This was a rough place full of even rougher men who had come to enjoy their vices with no care for the law of God or man.

Hendricks put his hand on her shoulder. 'We will take a table in the corner, out of the way of this mob. And I will enquire after him for you.' He led her to the corner, and a barmaid brought two mugs to the table with a sneer on her face. Emily glanced into hers to see that it was already filled. She smelled juniper.

Hastings placed a hand over her glass. 'The strength of the gin will not make up for the dirtiness of the glass.' He tossed a coin on the table. As the barmaid reached for it, he caught her by the wrist. 'The Earl of Folbroke. Do you know him? Is he here?' The girl shook her head, but he did not release her. 'Do you know an Adrian Longesley?'

'Addy?' She gave a single nod, and he let go of her arm, but his action had drawn the eyes of others.

The men who rose from the nearest table were hulking brutes, looking for any reason to fight. 'Here now, stranger. You have a dollymop of your own, do you not?' The one who spoke gave Emily a toothless leer.

'Aye,' said another. 'If you wish to share our Molly, then you must share as well.' Behind her, a man leaned close, and she inched her chair away.

'Now, see here.' Hendricks's gaze was steely, and his shoulders broad. Though she thought him timid when compared to Adrian, he had been a captain in the army, and she had no doubt that he would defend her honour to the best of his considerable abilities. But with so many against him, she doubted that his strength would do them much good.

And as she feared, when Hendricks started to rise, a fist to his jaw knocked him back into the chair.

She gave a little shriek of alarm as one of the men crowding the table reached for her. This had been a dreadful mistake. The place was horrible, the men were horrible, and what was likely to happen now would be the fault of her own stupidity. Even if her husband was here, she doubted she wanted to see him. If he were part of the crowd around her, he was most likely beyond redemption.

And then, as she gave another cry of alarm, a hand reached out through the press of bodies around her chair, seized her by the arm and pulled her forwards until she was crushed against the body of her rescuer.

Chapter Three

*'C*an't you see that she does not wish your company?' A silver-headed cane shot out, rapping one man upon the head and another across the knuckles. The men who were struck gave sharp cries of pain, and grumbled as their fellows laughed at their distress.

Emily wrapped her arms about the waist of the man who held her to keep from swooning with relief. She recognised the voice of her husband, and was more gratified to be close to him than she had been at any time since the day of their marriage.

'And you think she wants you instead?' a man called. There was a chorus of laughter from around the room.

'How can she not?' Adrian called back. 'I am the only gentleman amongst you.'

More laughter in response.

'And she is clearly a lady of discerning taste, if she has the sense enough to reject you.'

There was yet more laughter to this, and she could not decide if it was directed to Adrian, or to the fact that she had been called a lady.

There was a pause, as she wondered if he meant to answer the insults to her with anything more than jests. Then he turned her to face him.

He had changed, of course, but not so much that she could not recognise him. His coat was of good quality, but ragged and dirty. His neckcloth was stained and his dark brown hair needed combing. But he still had shockingly blue eyes, though they gave her little more than a sidelong glance. And there was the roguish smile that he shared with other women more often than he did with her. His body was just as strong and solid as it had ever been, so muscular that she felt dwarfed against him as he held her close. Frightened of being crushed, and yet still protected.

She could feel her nerve failing now that he was close, and the growing desire to sink into him, soaking in the warmth of his body as though immersed in the bath. What was around them did not matter. She was with Adrian. She would be all right.

And then he kissed her. On the mouth.

The suddenness of it shocked her. She had expected a distant greeting, and his customary slight frown, as though, even as he was saying hello, he was thinking of ways to say goodbye.

But he was kissing her. They were really kissing. And it was like nothing she had experienced before. He tasted of gin and tobacco, smelled of sweat, and his cheeks were rough with several days' beard growth. It was a sensory onslaught: a strange combination of the pleasant and the unpleasant. Joyful. Abandoned. And wet.

His kisses of the past had been unmemorable. Reserved. Flavourless and without texture. And much as she had wanted to feel otherwise, she had not liked them very much. He had been so careful to give no offence that he could not have enjoyed them either. Even in consummation, he had set himself apart from her, allowing no loss of self-control.

But today, in a crowded tavern, without asking her leave or showing a care to the men watching them, he devoured her mouth as he might a piece of late-summer fruit, giving a low *hmmm* of approval at the ripeness, the juiciness. He clutched her bottom through her skirts, and eased a leg between her parting thighs, giving her a small bounce there, to make sure that he had shaken her to the core.

And for a moment she forgot her anger with him and her fear. All the feelings of hurt and betrayal disappeared, along with the shyness she felt when she was with him. After all this time, he had decided he loved her. He wanted her. And if she could have him back, just like this, everything would be all right.

Then he pulled away and whispered in her ear, 'Here now, love. Nothing to be frightened of. Let us leave these brigands behind. Come and sit on my lap.'

'I beg your pardon.' The happy thoughts froze in her head, and cold logic returned to its proper place. The request was odd, and delivered in a way that showed a strange lack of feeling for his friend and servant, Hendricks, struggling back to consciousness in the chair in front of him.

Adrian gave her another small hug and a quick kiss on the lips to coax her. 'You may help me with my cards tonight. There will be a shiny sovereign for you, if you are good.' He said it as if he were talking to a stranger. There was no trace of recognition in that voice. No hint that this was to be a shared joke, or a lark or that he was trying to protect her from the ruffians by hiding her identity.

Was he honestly so drunk that he did not know her?

'Help you with your cards?' she said. The last haze of desire cleared from her mind. If he did not claim her as wife, then just who had he thought he'd been kissing? 'I should think you could manage them without my help, just as you normally do, my lord.'

The censure in her voice did not seem to register. 'You would be surprised, my dear.' He was whispering in her ear. 'It seems I need more help by the day.' He kissed her on the side of the head, as though to confirm to the others that he was whispering endearments, and then said more loudly, 'Since we are to be fast friends, you may call me Adrian.' And then he pulled her away from the crowd, stumbling back towards a gaming table on the other side of the room.

Emily struggled against him, trying to catch her breath long enough to argue that this behaviour was an insult worse than any she had yet borne. But he conquered her easily and sat down on a chair with his back to the wall, drawing her into his lap. And all the time he continued to kiss the side of her face and her neck, as though he could not get enough of the contact.

The feel of his lips, hot on her skin, made her anger seem distant and unimportant. If he could not overcome this sudden desire to touch her, then why should she? His body knew her, even if his mind did not. She arched her back and pressed her cheek against his lips, vowing that while they had differences to settle, surely it could wait a while longer...

And then he whispered in a calm voice, unaffected by the nearness of her, 'They will deal a hand to me, and you must read the pips on the cards into my ear. Pretend it is merely affection, just as I have done to you. Help me to know the cards that are played. And as I promised, you shall have your sovereign.'

'Pretend?' Was that all this was to him?

'Shh,' he whispered, lips still against her jaw. 'A guinea, then.'

Her anger returned. He was nothing more than she believed him to be: a drunken reprobate who could think no further than his own pleasure. And she was a fool who could not conquer the fantasies she had created around him, no matter how many times he showed his true face to her.

And with the anger came curiosity. He still did not know her. But it seemed his seduction was just as much a sham for the stranger he thought he held. He seemed to care more for the cards than he had for the kisses. And if that was true, his actions made no sense at all to her.

So she did just as he had requested, hoping the motive would become clear with time. He held her close as the hands were dealt, and she whispered a description of the play into his ear.

Emily watched the men across the table from her, certain that they must have some idea of what was going on, for they kept their eyes on her, and their hands tilted carefully towards them, as though fearing that she might be attempting to read what was concealed there.

But her husband did not seem to notice the fact, nor care what the others might hold. He greeted each new hand with a vacuous and unfocused smile, head tilted slightly to one side so that he might concentrate on the words she whispered in his ear.

As she watched, she began to suspect that it was not his smile that was unfocused. It was the look in his eyes. He looked not on her, or the cards before him—not even the men across the table. It was as though he were peering through the space around him, a little to the left, at some spot near the floor, expecting an invisible door would open a view to another place entirely. Was he drunk, or was it something far worse?

Despite his strange behaviour, his mind was still sharp. After a single recitation of information, he had no trouble keeping his hand straight, nor with bidding or points. He won more than he lost. And then he ran his hands once over the winnings heaped in front of him, conscious of any move to cheat him out of what should rightfully come to his side of the table, reaching for his cane and tapping it sharply on the floor to emphasise his disapproval, if what he found was not to his liking.

She saw the wary look that the men around them gave to that stick and its heavy silver head, and the speed with which they put an end to any mischief when Adrian reached for it. They seemed to view it and her husband not with fear, but with a sort of grudging respect, as though experience had taught them he was an opponent who would not be easily bested.

After a time, Adrian seemed to tire of play, shifting her on his lap as though he grew restless. 'Enough, gentlemen,' he said with a smile, pulling the money before him to the edge of the table and into a purse he removed from his coat. He gave a theatrical yawn and turned his head to hers again and said, 'I am of a mind to retire for the evening.' And then, 'If you would be so kind as to accompany me, I will give you the coin I promised.'

He pocketed the purse and his hand went back to her waist, and then up, stroking the underside of her breast through the fabric of her dress.

She gave a little yelp of alarm, embarrassed by his forwardness, and slapped his fingers away. 'Please do not do that.'

The men around them laughed, and she kept her eyes firmly on the table, not wanting to see what Hendricks thought of this public affront upon her person.

Nor did she wish him to see the flush of excitement on her cheeks. Though she did not want to feel anything from it, her husband's touch was arousing her. It was probably just as well that he did not know her. If he had, he would have stood up, spoken politely and taken her by the arm instead of the waist. Then he would have rushed her back to the country so that her presence in London would not have spoiled his fun.

Instead, she could feel the hardness beneath her bottom, and the way her denial of him had made his response more urgent. He buried his face in the hollow of her throat, inhaling deeply and licking once at her collarbone. 'I cannot help my reaction. You smell wonderful.'

'And you do not.' She shook him off, sitting up straighter, angered by his weakness and her own.

Adrian gave a sharp laugh, and it was honest mirth, as though he had not expected to be matched in wit by a doxy. He gave a sniff at his coat, as though gauging his own unpleasantness. 'Once I get out of these clothes, you will find I am not so bad.'

Although she doubted the fact, she nodded. It would be better to hold her temper for just a little while, for there was much that needed to be said, and she had no wish to do it in front of this rough audience. If she could get him to leave the place willingly, it would achieve her ends, and would be easier for both of them when difficult revelations had to be made.

He cocked his head to the side, not acknowledging her agreement, and so she said, 'Of course, Adrian. Lead the way.'

He pushed her bottom and slid her out of his lap, then stood and reached for his stick. And she noticed with a grim certainty that he did not lean upon the cane for support, nor swagger with it, as though it was a mere ornament. Instead, he used it to part the crowd around the table, letting it tap idly along the ground as he walked. And instead of going towards the front door and freedom, he walked farther into the tavern, towards the stairs at the back of the room.

Emily pulled on his sleeve and said through clenched teeth, 'My lord, did you not wish to leave this place?'

He took her arm, pulling her along with him. 'I have let space here. It is easier, after a long night of play.' He kissed her again, thrusting his tongue once deep into her mouth, until her mind went blank. 'And much closer.' When they reached the steps he put his hand on the rail, sheltering her body between his and the wall. As they started to climb, she turned back to Hendricks, who still sat by the door, giving him a helpless look and hoping that he had some wisdom or explanation to offer.

Instead, he gave a small shrug in answer, as though to tell her that this was her plan, not his. He would wait upon her orders to decide the next action.

So she shook her head and held up a staying hand, hoping that he would understand that she meant to follow Adrian, at least for now. There was no point in explaining her identity to him in this crush. It would be embarrassing enough when they were alone.

It was then she saw a body breaking from the throng below, running for the stairs. An angry loser from the gaming table had waited until Adrian's back was turned and was coming after them, his arm raised in threat.

Her husband cocked his head at the sound of running

footsteps on the treads behind them; without a word, he switched his stick to his other hand, turned and brought the thing down on the head of his adversary. Then he gave a shove backwards with it, knocking the other man off balance and sending him down the stairs.

'Idiot,' he muttered. 'I shall take my play elsewhere, if this is how they wish to behave here. What he thought to accomplish by that, I have no idea. He should know damn well that I am blind, not deaf.'

Chapter Four

'Blind?' She should not have been surprised, for it had been obvious as she'd sat with him that he could not read the cards in his hand, nor recognise his own wife, though she sat in his lap.

He smiled, not the least bit bothered by it. 'Not totally. Not yet, at least. I can see shapes. And light and dark. And enough of you to know that you are a more attractive companion than that blighter I just knocked down the stairs. But I fear that cards are quite beyond my scope.'

'But how?'

'You are a curious one, aren't you?' He climbed the rest of the stairs with her, opening the door at their head and leading her down the gloomy corridor behind it. 'It is a family condition, aggravated by a war injury. There was a flash, you see. And I was too close. Without that, I might have lasted a good long time with these tired old eyes. A lifetime, perhaps. Or perhaps not. Not all the men of my family have the problem. I understand that it can take some time before the world begins to go dark.'

'But I never knew.' And his family had lived beside hers for generations.

'A blind man?' He smiled, and turned suddenly, pushing her against the wall and pinning her hands above her head with his ebony walking stick. Then he kissed her again, more ardently than he had at any point in their brief time together. His lips were on her mouth, her cheeks, her chin, her throat. And she felt the delicious loss of control she'd felt when he kissed her below stairs, and nothing had mattered but the moment they were sharing. He sagged against her so that he could suck and bite at the tops of her breasts, where they were exposed above the neckline of her gown, as though he could not wait a moment longer to bare them, and take the nipples between his lips. It made her moan in frustration, arching her back, struggling against the wood that held her in place and kept her from giving herself to him. It did not matter that he could not see who he was kissing. It was Adrian, and he wanted her. And, at last, she would have him the way she'd always imagined, the way she had wanted him for as long as she'd known the reason for kissing.

He gave a slight buck of his hips so she could feel what their kisses had done to him. And she felt her own wet heat rising in response at the memories of hardness and length and welcome penetration, and the panting eagerness to be so possessed.

And then he said in a voice that was not nearly flustered enough, 'It is only the eyes that are the problem. The rest of me is quite healthy, I assure you. Once we snuff the candles, you will find me much like any other man.'

Like any other man? For her, there had never been another. But what was happening to him was so common he was barely affected by it. Her eyes flew open and she stared past his shoulder, aware of their shabby surroundings and remembering the reason that she had come looking for him. He had treated her abominably since the day they had married. And now, after a few kisses she had forgotten it all, willing to be used in a public hallway like one of his whores. 'Let go of me. This instant. Release my arms, you beast, or I shall scream to bring down the roof.' She struggled against his lips, against his body and against the stick that stayed her hands.

He stepped back and lowered his cane, a slight puzzled frown upon his face. 'Are you sure? There is a private room just down the hall. The door locks, and only I have the key. We will be all alone, with no fear of interruption.' He paused, and then his lips twitched into a coaxing smile. 'I can give you the guinea I promised. There is more than enough from the table tonight. You should know for you saw it. I can tell money well enough, one coin from another,' he assured hurriedly, as though assuming this might be the problem. 'They feel differently in weight and size. And as for the rest of it?' He stepped close again. And when she did not pull away he dipped his head and began to kiss her again, slowly working his way down her throat to settle on the hollow of her shoulder. Then he moved just enough so his lips were no longer touching her, then spoke and let his breath do the teasing. 'I have been assured that the reliance on other senses has made me an unusually observant lover. I particularly value touch in these moments, and use it to good advantage. And taste.' He licked with just the lip of his tongue, as though he were sampling her flavour.

Emily gave another dizzy shudder; she could swear that she felt that single lick to the very core of her body, making her imagine he was kissing her in a place that was most unlikely and very improper. And she wondered, would he be shocked if she suggested such a thing?

Or had he been doing that, and worse? He had been assured of his prowess, had he? *Assured by whom?* She buried her fingers in his hair, trying to pull him away, focusing on the last three years, the doubt, the loneliness, the anger. Had he been going blind, even from the first? Had he known when they married? Had he hurried to marry a foolish woman who was oblivious to his disability?

And what had he been doing since he left her?

Adrian gave a small grunt of pain from the tugging on his hair and lifted his face as if to gaze at her, but in the same sidelong way he looked at everything that told her he could not really see. 'The coin I offered is still yours, for services rendered at the gaming table. But now that we are above—' he gave a small shrug '—if you do not think it sufficient, I am open to discussion on the subject.'

She balled her fist and gave him a clout upon the ear. 'I am not a whore, you cloth-brained drunkard. And even if I was, I would not lie with you for all the money in the world.'

The blow did not faze him at all. And the insults made him laugh. But he released her with a bow. 'Then I apologise for my mistake, though I can hardly be blamed for it. If you are not a whore, then what are you doing in a place such as this?'

It was a fair question, and even she did not know the whole answer to it. At last she said, 'I was searching for someone.' She stared at him, willing him to recognise her. 'For my husband.'

'And I assume, since you are alone here with me that you did not find him?'

'No, I did not.' For the man before her, although right in appearance, was as far away from the man she'd thought she married as was possible. A little bit of her anger gave way to disappointment. And then she felt the growing heat of embarrassment. If he was already amused, how hard would he laugh to realise that he had wasted kisses on his own wife?

'I should have recognised that you were a lady of breeding earlier by the tone of your voice.' He sighed, and tapped his forehead with the head of his cane. 'Perhaps the gin has finally addled my brains. But when you came upstairs with me, I was under the impression…'

He cleared his throat and grinned, allowing her to fill in the rest.

'You might not be able to see where you gamble, but I have the misfortune of two good eyes. I foolishly blundered into a place that was not safe for me. You came to my rescue, and I thought that, unlike the other men here, if I got you alone it would be possible to reason with you. Which I am doing, now.' Though he could not appreciate the fact, she reached to straighten her hair and clothing, trying to erase the signs of her earlier compliance.

'Well. Never mind what I assumed.' He gave another little clearing of the throat. 'The less spoken of that the better. I was wrong, and I am sorry if I have given offence. If there is a way I can be of assistance, then, please, tell me.' It was as if, with a few sentences, he thought to regain his honour and pretend the last few minutes had not occurred.

Emily did not know whether to be angry, or impressed by the transformation. From beneath them, she could hear the men in the tavern growing louder, angrier and possibly more dangerous. Perhaps now was not the best time to tell her husband what she thought of his behaviour, and his quick about-face turn on the subject of her virtue. 'If you wish to help me, then take me away from here. It is a bad place, full of violent, drunken men. Is there some back stairway that we can use to escape?'

He shook his head. 'The only way out is to go back the way we came.'

'You allowed us to be trapped upstairs?' This was certainly not the sharp military strategy she had expected from a former officer of his Majesty's army. 'Whatever were you thinking to take a room here? You might be able to fight them tonight, but some day the ruffians you gamble with will catch you unawares and make an end to you.'

He shrugged and fumbled to pat her on the arm. 'Of course, my dear. I fully expect that to be the truth.'

She stared at him in amazement, and then realised that her shocked expression was useless as a way to covey her emotions. 'Then why are you here?'

'Because soon, the last of my vision will go, and I will be of no use to the world. Better to go out doing things that I enjoy, than to put a bullet in my head at the first sign of trouble. That is the way, in my family. My father died on horseback.' He grinned. 'Or just off it, actually. A snapped spine and a crushed body. But he loved to ride. And up till the end, he was sailing over jumps that he could no longer see. My grandfather was a crack shot. Until the day he missed, at least.' He grinned as though it were a point of admiration. 'Killed in a duel. Over a woman, of course.'

And hadn't that been what she had always known about her husband and his family? But her brother had assured her that Adrian was *wild like all the Folbrokes. But with a good heart, Emily. A very good heart.*

'And you?'

'I am a soldier,' he added. 'And well used to drinking and gaming in rough company. If the night ends in a scrap? I like nothing better. When the odds are bad, it gets the blood flowing in the veins.' He seemed to swell a little at the thought as though readying himself for battle.

'And now, because of your foolish desire for self-destruction, I will end my night at the mercy of the gang below.'

He stilled, and then something in him straightened, as though he could cast off the inebriate as easily as throwing off his coat. And for a moment, in the dark, he was the dashing young man who had gone off to war, only to return and break her heart. Then he smiled. It was the old smile, too, unclouded by gin or lust. Brave. Beautiful. And a little sad. 'Have I not proved to you already that I am still capable of taking care of myself, and you as well? Or is another demonstration in order?'

Although he could not see, he looked at her with such intensity that the pain inside her did not seem to matter. There was something in that gaze and that smile that said any action he might take was likely to be a great adventure, and that it would be his pleasure to share it with her. It made her heart flutter in the way it used to, before he had married her, and before she had learned what a mistake it was all likely to be.

'Perhaps it would be better if we wait in the room you mentioned, until it is safe to depart.' She could hear her nerve failing again, and her voice becoming weak. The old hesitant Emily was returning with her husband's gain in sobriety.

He laughed. 'I have done nothing yet to earn such intimacy from you, pleasant though the offer might be. But if you stay just behind me as we descend, I can get you to safety. Hang on to my coat tails and leave my hands free, for I may need to fight.'

'But you cannot see,' she said plaintively.

'I do not need to. I know the way out. And I intend to hit anyone who stands between me and the door. Those that mean us no harm will have the sense to get out of the way.'

Emily had no answer for this, having no experience with fighting one's way out of a tavern. So she took his coat tail in her hands, and followed close behind him down the stairs. As they breached the upper landing, she could tell from the sounds below them that the crowd had grown worse. There was more chanting, a raucous edge to the singing, the scuffling of boots and fists, and breaking furniture.

Adrian paused, listening. 'What do you see before you? Quickly, love.'

'Two men are fighting on a table to the right.'

'Very good.' He continued down the stairs, hugging the wall as he worked his way towards the door. As the fight spilled off the table and into his path, he struck out with the cane, just as he'd said he would. The first blow was a glancing one, causing the man in front of him to yelp and cringe back.

But the second man surged forwards as though willing to fight both his supposed enemy and any other that might stand against him. Adrian forced the stick forwards quickly, jabbing into the man's midsection.

The drunkard retched, and then flailed out, trying to strike. Adrian brought the stick down upon the man's back so hard that, for a moment, Emily feared the wood had cracked.

He stepped over the man's prone body, reaching back to steady her. But the momentary distraction over her safety was enough to make him jeopardise his own. Out of the corner of her eye, she caught the flash of a raised hand, and saw the man that had accosted them on the stairs throw a bottle up and out from the throng in the middle of the room.

Before she could get out a warning, Adrian had been struck, and was staggering backwards, clutching his temple. His body went limp in her arms as she tried to catch him.

Chapter Five

Then there was a flash toward the ceiling and the sound of a warning shot. Her husband's secretary appeared out of nowhere to pull Adrian forwards again, and off her. In his usual quiet way, Hendricks said, 'I apologise for not intervening until this delicate juncture. But I am sure that my lord would have preferred it thus. And now I think it best that we make a retreat while we are able.' He pressed a second pistol into her hand. 'I doubt this will be necessary now that I have frightened them. But it is better to be over-prepared.'

He pushed her husband back against the wall for a moment, and then slung the limp body over his shoulder, staggering towards the door to the street.

Emily held the pistol in front of her, hoping that she did not look as frightened by it as she felt. But it appeared to be effective. The man who'd hit Adrian had been preparing to strike again. At the sight of the gun he took a large step back, his anger dissolving into submission.

Hendricks lurched through the door and towards the waiting coach. When he saw them, the coachman rushed forwards to help his unconscious master up and into the carriage.

As they set off, poor Adrian remained slumped against the squabs, rendered insensible by the combination of violence and gin. It was not until they were nearly back to his rooms that he surged suddenly back to consciousness, throwing a hand out as though searching the air in front of him. 'Hendricks?'

'Yes, my lord.'

'There was a woman in the tavern with me. I was trying to help her.'

'She is safe, sir.'

He relaxed back into the seat, with a sigh of relief and a grimace of pain. 'Very good.'

Once they arrived at the flat, she followed behind as the men helped him up the stairs. She noted the looks of alarm on the faces of his servants as they saw her appear from behind him. Clearly, the jig was up and they expected punishment from her for concealing the state of things, or from Adrian for revealing them.

As she passed them, she shot them glares that would warn them to silence.

Hendricks gave her a helpless shrug, opening the bedroom door and putting his arm around the shoulders of his employer. 'The valet will help him from here, mmm—ma'am.' He struggled a moment to choose an honourific, as though remembering that he apparently did not know the name of the woman who had come home with them. 'I will find someone to see you home.'

When she was sure that her husband would see the shadow of her head, she nodded in approval. Then she backed from the room and shut the door.

'Hendricks,' she kept her voice low, so that it would not carry to the bedroom, but used a tone of command that had served her well when dealing with employees who thought, even for a moment, that they owed more loyalty to her husband than to the woman standing in front of them.

'My lady.' She saw his spine stiffen instantly to full obedience.

She glared at him. 'You did not tell me.'

'That he was blind? I thought you knew.'

She was his wife. She should have known that about him, if nothing else. But what was one more regret on a very long list? But now, Hendricks mocked her ignorance.

Then, as a sop to her feelings, he said, 'The servants are not allowed to discuss Lord Folbroke's indisposition. He pretends it does not matter. Often it does not. But he acts as if the careless things he does pose no greater risk to him. He is very wrong.'

She had to agree, for it was quite obviously true. 'Between the drink, and the loss of vision, he did not know me.'

'Yes, my lady.' Hendricks did not seem surprised. But

she felt some gratification to see that he looked ashamed of his part in the state of things.

'It will save us both embarrassment if that is the way this night remains. You will inform the servants that, no matter what they might think they have seen, he was brought home by a stranger. Is that clear?'

'Yes, Lady Folbroke.'

'When I have had time to think on this, I will have some words with him. But it must wait until my husband's mind has cleared itself of blue ruin.'

The secretary's reserve broke. 'While I have no doubt that you will achieve the first half of the statement, the last may be beyond all of our control.' Then, as though he could mitigate the forwardness of the statement, he added, 'My lady.' And then he gave her a desperate look as though it pained him to betray the confidence. 'He is seldom sober any more. Even during the day. We who have served him for most of his life are at our wits' end as to what can be done.'

Emily thought of the man in the other room, reeking of gin. Was it really so different than what she had feared? In her heart, she had been sure that she would find him drunk. But she had mistaken the reason. She reached out to touch the arm of the man beside her. 'How long has he been like this?'

'The whole of the last month, certainly.' He tapped his forehead. 'It is the eyes, my lady. As they fail him, he loses all hope. My lord's valet has heard him laugh and say that it will not be a problem for long. We fear he means to do something desperate. And we do not know how to stop him.'

She closed her own eyes and took a deep breath, telling herself that this was an estate matter, nothing more. Her heart was no longer involved in it. She must remember her reasons for coming to find him, and that they had nothing to do with a reconciliation or delivering scolds about his scandalous conduct.

But no matter how she felt about his treatment of her, she could not very well allow him to kill himself.

'My husband has taken the notion that this is for the best. I can see, as plainly as you can, that this is nonsense. He is not thinking clearly, and I will not allow him to do himself an injury. At least not until he can present a better reason than the minor problem he has.'

Or until I am sure that my own place is secure.

If he was truly resolved to end his life, she doubted that there was anything to be done. She was little better than a stranger to him. What would he care what she thought? She hardened her heart against the desperation and panic that she was feeling. 'My orders stand, just as they are. You and the other servants are forbidden from speaking of my efforts to find Adrian, or my return with him this evening. Let him think me a stranger.' Then she pushed past the secretary and went into her husband's room.

The valet looked terrified by her sudden appearance, and she held up a hand as a sign of caution. Then she looked down at the man on the bed who was now dressed in a nightshirt, and sporting a makeshift bandage on his temple. 'Before I left, I wished to assure myself that you are all right.'

At the sound of her voice he looked pained that she had found him helpless. There was a lost look in his blank blue eyes that made him seem smaller than she knew him to be. 'It should not be your job to see to my safety. As a gentleman, I should have been able to take care of you.'

'You succeeded,' she said. 'You fought well. We were within a few feet of the door when you were struck down. And that was by an unfair blow. A sighted man could not have done better and would have ended just as you did.'

There was a ghost of his old, rakish smile, as he tried to joke away his embarrassment. 'My talents do not end there, my dear.' He patted the bed at his side. 'If you wish to come closer, I would be happy to demonstrate.'

'That will not be necessary.' She paused long enough to see the slightest crease of disappointment form on his forehead. 'I prefer my companions to be washed and shaved. And not soaked in gin. However...'

She leaned in to give him a peck on the forehead as a farewell reward. But as she did so, she realised that the token kiss would be everything he feared about his future. What she had intended as comfort would seem a sexless and maternal gesture, a cruel dismissal to the man who had fought to protect her.

So she pushed back upon his chest, forcing him into the pillows, and kissed him properly on the mouth. His lips opened in surprise, and she threw caution to the winds and slipped her tongue between them, stroking the inside of his mouth as he had done to hers. She felt the same rush of excitement she had felt in the tavern, and the desire to be closer still. And the feeling that she had felt often, over the last few years: that something was missing from her well-ordered life—and that, perhaps, it was Adrian Longesley.

Then she ended the kiss and turned to leave.

'Wait.' He caught her wrist.

'I must go.'

'You cannot. Not after that.'

She gave a little laugh. 'Neither can I stay.'

'Meet me again.' He ran his other hand through his hair in exasperation and his words were hurried, as though he was trying to think of anything that might tempt her to stay. 'So that I might assure myself of your safety, when I am not indisposed.' His smile was back again. 'You will like me better when I have had time to wash, dress and shave.'

'Will I have to go to a brothel to find you? Or merely a gaming hell?' She shook her head, and remembered that he would not see her refusal, then said, 'I think not.'

'Why not here? Tomorrow morning.'

'You expect me to come to a man's rooms, in daylight and unescorted.'

His face fell. 'Your reputation. I had forgotten.'

'Thank you very much for your belated concern.'

He winced as though it were a physical effort to stumble through the courtesies she deserved. 'If there were somewhere that we could talk, in privacy and discretion…'

Emily sighed, as though she were not sure of the wisdom of her actions and then let herself be persuaded. 'I will send you a letter, and you will come to me when it is convenient.'

He released her hand, letting his fingers drag down the length of it until he touched only her fingertips. 'I look forward to your communication.'

She was glad that he could not clearly see her. Had he not been blind, he would know that her cheeks were crimson and that the expression on her face was not the sly smile of a courtesan, but goggle-eyed amazement. Her husband looked forward to meeting with *her*. Before she could spoil the moment by saying something inappropriate, she turned and left.

It was not until she was in the carriage, on the way back to her brother's town house, that she allowed herself to collapse, then glared across the coach at Hendricks. 'How long have you known?'

'From the first. It came on gradually, after we left Portugal. He insisted that I tell you nothing. And although you and I have had reason to work together, he is, first and foremost, my employer. I must obey his wishes before yours.'

'I see.' Therefore, Hendricks was not to be trusted. She felt a cold chill at the loss of one she had trusted almost as a brother since the day she'd married Adrian. But if he could keep hidden a fact this momentous, then there was no telling what other secrets he'd hidden from her. 'So you meant to take the man's pay and allow him to destroy himself, when a word to me might have prevented it?'

Hendricks was embarrassed almost to the point of pain. 'I did not think it my place.'

'Then you had best reassess your position.' She took the stern, almost manly tone she used with him to indicate that she spoke for her husband and that disobedience was out of the question.

'Of course, my lady.'

She had cowed him, and it made her feel better, more in control than she had since the moment she had realised that she must see Adrian again.

But on the inside, she was unsure whether to laugh or to cry. It had finally happened, just as she'd dreamed of it, since she was a girl. Tonight, the man she loved had looked at her with desire, hung upon her every word and clung to her fingertips as though parting with her was an agony.

Of course, he was drunk, blind and did not know who she was. And the whole thing had happened so long after it should have that the point was moot. It had been nothing more than a girlish fantasy to have the dashing Earl of Folbroke dote on her like a love-struck fool. But then, she had thought that wedding him would mean something other than the sterile arrangement it was. Time had proven to her that he had no feelings for her, or he'd have been home long before now. 'I suspect the reason he found me so appealing is because he thought me married to someone else.'

'Lady Folbroke!' It was an exclamation of shock at her candour, but not one of denial. She feared it was a sign that Hendricks knew her husband only too well. She would return in the morning, when he was sober, and tell him what she thought of this nonsense. Disability was no excuse for the way he'd behaved. If he was not careful, he was likely to kill himself. Where would that leave her?

And if Adrian died, then she might never know…

Tomorrow, he would be hoping for a clandestine meeting, where they could be alone to talk. Ha. When she saw him next, she would talk aplenty. She would tell him what an idiot he was for not knowing her, and for thinking that his good looks and easy manner would be enough to make her forget his abandonment and let him bed her.

A delicious thrill went through her at the thought of being bedded, and she stifled it. It seemed there was no end to her foolishness over the man. She had known from the first that he was a rake. That knowledge should have provided some insulation against his charm. But his kisses made her wonder what it might be like, should he turn his full attention to winning her, even for a few hours.

And it might be the only way to get an heir by him. That was what she had wanted, above all. It was her reason for coming to London.

Emily stared at Hendricks, eyes narrowing and chin

set to remind him that she was the Countess of Folbroke, and not some silly schoolgirl. She deserved his respect every bit as much as her wayward husband. 'Adrian is sorely mistaken if he thinks to keep me in darkness about events any longer. And you are as big a fool as he, for helping him this long. I will not condone his drinking, or support this lunatic notion he has that being struck down in a common brawl is the way to meet his Maker on his own terms. But if a liaison with another man's wife is what he desires, then I see no reason not to give it to him.'

She smiled and watched Hendricks draw away from her in alarm. 'And how do you mean to do that?'

'I mean to return to my brother and do nothing at all. But you will have a busy day tomorrow, Mr Hendricks. I wish you to engage a flat for me while I am in London. Something simple, small. *A pied-à-terre.* Decoration does not matter, since my guest will not see it. I will need staff as well. Choose what is necessary from our household, or hire if you must, but I will have no gossip. They will speak not so much as a word to identify themselves to Lord Folbroke, or I will sack the lot of them. Is that understood?'

'Yes, my lady.' Clearly, the actions were not understood at all. Judging by the look on his face, he found them to be incomprehensible. But he knew better than to cross her, and that was enough.

'When that is completed, and not before, you will take a note to my husband. And you will give him no indication of my involvement in it, or I swear, Mr Hendricks, that no matter what my husband might say in the matter, you will be seeking other employment before the sun sets. Is that clear?'

'Yes, Lady Folbroke.' There was a trace of awe in his tone. But she also recognised the relief in it, as though he understood that, if she were allowed to take the reins, they would all be the better for it. His obedience was gratifying, and yet strangely disappointing. She was tired of being surrounded by men that presented no real challenge to her authority.

But she suspected that she would be regretting the lack of just that by tomorrow evening. It made her tremble when she thought of the kiss Adrian had given her, and the kiss she had given him in return. She had never felt such power in her life and yet utterly in the thrall of another. The man she'd kissed had wanted to be seduced by her as much as he'd wanted to take her. And, for a moment, she had wanted the same.

Tomorrow, on neutral ground, they would meet. She would invite. He would accept. She would feign *naïveté*. He would suggest. She would protest. He would cajole. She would be persuaded. The conclusion might be inevitable, but for a time there would be a battle of wits and wills leading to both a complete surrender and an equally complete victory. If handled correctly, there would be ecstasy, satisfaction and sweet, sweet revenge.

Across from her in the carriage, Hendricks looked quite unsettled by the latest turn of events. But with regard to Adrian, Emily had never felt so confident in her life. As soon as all things were in place, she would go about the tawdry, ridiculous and strangely exhilarating process of ensnaring her own husband.

Chapter Six

Adrian Longesley awoke the next day with the same nagging, drunkard's headache he had grown accustomed to. A morning would come soon enough when he did not wake at all. In comparison, it would be a welcome relief. But today, he was alive and conscious, and feeling the worse for a lump on his forehead. If he had been coshed from behind, he'd have felt better about the injury. But to be hit from the front with a blow that had seemed to come from nowhere proved how far his abilities had diminished. He sighed into the pillow, waiting for the rolling of the room to subside enough so that he might sit up.

The nausea would probably be worse if he could see the movement. Even without that particular sense, he was sure that he could feel the rocking, as though he were making a rough crossing to France. But he was still in his own bedchamber, and could smell a breakfast he had no appetite for.

The woman.

He had been a drunken fool to think he'd be lucky enough to rescue her twice from the place he'd found her. If his carelessness had allowed her to fall into the hands of the men there…

He lurched upright in panic, and then regretted it, before remembering the end of the evening. He had a hazy recollection of her voice on the carriage ride home, along with that of Hendricks. His man must have found him in time, saved the girl and helped them to return here.

It pained him further that he had needed rescuing at all. If he had fallen to a place where he could no longer care for himself and put innocents around him at risk, then it might be time to seek a sudden end to things and stop dawdling about, waiting for nature to take its course. But last night had not been the time. The strange woman had needed him, if only for a short time. If the intervention of Hendricks had assured her safety, then his own pride could survive the damage of needing assistance.

She had claimed to be well bred, and gentle, though she certainly hadn't been wise. A wise woman would never come to such a place. Maybe what she'd said was true, and she'd actually been looking for her husband. Sad for her, if that was the sort of place she might find him. While Adrian shared it, it was nothing to be proud of. But at least he had the small comfort of knowing that his wife had never seen it.

The stranger had refused him, when they'd been alone. So it was not a visit brought on by a secret desire to slum for the novelty of it. And then she had followed him back to his house. She had been in this very bed-chamber, though not for long enough. He remembered her assurances that he had fought well for her, and the tiniest hint of awe in her sceptical voice.

She had been tart in manner and in kisses. And scent as well, for he could swear that the smell of lemons still clung to his skin where she had touched him. What a woman she had been. If his memory could be trusted, he'd have been happy to have more of her company. The round, soft way she had felt in his lap, and the tingling friction of her tongue in his mouth. The pleasant weight of her breasts brushing his arm as she bent over his bed. And a kiss that hinted of more to come.

He laughed. Another meeting was unlikely, and per-haps impossible. She had promised, of course, to get him to release her hand. But she had not given him name or direction and had called him rough company. He rubbed at the stubble on his chin. She was probably right.

His valet must have heard him stirring, for Adrian could hear his entrance, and smell the morning cup of tea that he put on the bedside table and the soap that he carried as he went to the basin to prepare the water for washing and shaving. There was another set of footsteps, the scrape of curtain rings, and the sudden bright blur as the sun streamed into his bedroom. 'Hendricks,' he said, 'you are a beast. The least you could do is allow a man to adjust slowly to the morning.'

'Afternoon, my lord,' Hendricks responded politely. 'It is almost one o'clock.'

'And all the same to me. You know the hour I came home, and the condition I was in, for you brought me.' A thought occurred to him. 'And how did you come to do that? When I left here, I was alone.'

There was an awkward shifting of weight and clearing of throat. 'I came searching for you, my lord. While you were out, Lady Folbroke visited to inform you that she is staying in London. She was quite insistent to know your whereabouts. And I thought it best…'

'I see.' His wife had come to town before. And each time he had managed to avoid her. But it was damned awkward, after the events of last night, to think her so close. He reached for the miniature of Emily in its usual evening resting place on the table by the bed, fingering it idly.

'You had been out for some time, already,' Hendricks continued. 'The servants were concerned.'

The voice in Adrian's head snapped that it was no one's business what he did with his time. Their concern was nothing more than thinly veiled pity, and the suspicion that he could not be trusted to take care of himself. He held his temper. If one had been carried insensible out of a gin mill, it hardly gave one the right to argue that one was fine on one's own.

Instead, he said, 'Thank them for their concern, and thank you as well for your timely intervention. It was appreciated. I will try to be more careful in the future.'

In truth, he would be nothing of the kind. But there was no point in rubbing the man's nose in the fact.

And then, to make it appear an afterthought, he came back to the matter that concerned him most. 'But you said Emily is in town. Did you enquire as to the reason for the visit?'

'She did not say, my lord.' There was a nervous rustling of the papers in Hendricks's hands.

'You saw to the transfer of funds to the working accounts that we discussed after your last visit north?'

'Yes, my lord. Lady Folbroke inspected the damage from the spring storms, and repairs on the cottages are already underway.'

'I don't suppose it is that, then,' he said, trying not to be apprehensive. The efficiency of his wife was almost legendary. Hendricks had read the report she had written, explaining in detail the extent of the damage, her plans for repair and the budget she envisioned. The signature she'd required from him was little more than a courtesy on her part, to make him feel he was involved in the running of his lands.

But if she had come to London, and more importantly, come looking for him, the matter was likely to be of a much more personal nature. He remarked, as casually as possible, 'How is she?'

There was such a pause that he wondered if she was not well, or if there were something that they did not wish him to know. And then Hendricks said, 'She seemed well.'

'Emily has been on my mind often of late.' It was

probably the guilt. For he could swear that the scent of lemons still lingered in the room so strongly he feared Hendricks must smell it as well. 'Is there anything at all that she requires? More money, perhaps.'

'I am certain, if she required it, she would write herself a cheque from the household accounts.'

'Oh. Clothing, then. Does she shop frequently? I know my mother did. Perhaps she has come to town for that.'

'She has never complained of a lack,' he replied, as though the subject were tiresome and devoid of interest to him.

'Jewellery, then. She has received nothing since our wedding.'

'If you are interested, perhaps you should ask her yourself.' Hendricks said this sharply, as though despite his patient nature, he was growing frustrated by the endless questions.

'And did she mention whether she'd be likely to visit me again?' The question filled him with both hope and dread, as it always did. For though he would most like to see her again—as though that were even possible—he was not eager to hear what she would say if she learned the truth.

'I think she made some mention of setting up housekeeping here in London.' But Hendricks sounded more than unsure. He sounded as though he were keeping a secret from him. Possibly at his wife's request.

'Does she visit anyone else that you know of?' As if he had any right to be jealous, after all this time. But it would make perfect sense if she had found someone to entertain her in his absence. It had been three years. In the time since he'd left she would have blossomed to the prime of womanhood.

'Not that I know of, my lord. But she did mention your cousin Rupert.'

'Hmm.' He took a sip of his tea, trying to appear non-committal. Some would think it mercenary of her. But there was a kind of sense in it, he supposed, if she transferred her interests to the next Earl of Folbroke. When he was gone, she could keep her title, and her home as well. 'But Rupert…' he said, unable to keep from voicing his distaste of the man. 'I know he is family. But I had hoped she would have better taste.'

If he had eyes as strong as his fists, there would be no question of interference from his cousin in that corner. Even blind, he had a mind to give the man a thrashing, next time he came round to the flat. While he might forgive his wife an infidelity, crediting the fault to his own neglect of her, it would not do to let Rupert think she was part of the entail. She deserved better.

Not that she is likely to get it from you…

'It is not as if she shares the details of her personal life with the servants,' Hendricks interrupted his reverie. Was that meant as a prod to his conscience for asking questions that only he himself could learn the answers to?

Surely by now Hendricks must have guessed his real reasons for curiosity, and the utter impossibility of talking to Emily himself. 'It is none of my business either, I am sure. I have no real claim on her.'

'Other than marriage,' Hendricks pointed out in a dry tone.

'Since I have made no effort to be a good husband to her, it seems hypocritical to expect her continued loyalty to me. And if she has a reason to visit me again? If you could give me advance notice of the visit, I would be grateful. It would be better, if a meeting cannot be avoided, that it be prepared for.' On both sides. She deserved warning as well. He was in no condition, either physical or mental, to meet with her now.

'Very good, my lord.' Adrian could sense a lessening of the tension in the man beside the bed at the mention of even a possibility of a meeting. Acting as a go-between for them had been hard on his friend.

But now Hendricks was shifting again, as though there was some fresh problem. 'Is there some other news that brings you here?' he asked.

'The post has come,' Hendricks said, without expression.

'If I have slept past noon, I would hope it has. Is there something you wish to read to me?'

'A letter. It has no address, and the wax was unmarked. I took the liberty...'

'Of course.' Adrian waved away his concerns. 'Since I cannot see the words, my correspondence is as an open book to you. Please read the contents.' He set down his tea, took a piece of toast from the rack and waited.

Hendricks cleared his throat and read with obvious discomfort, 'I wish to thank you for your assistance on the previous evening. If you would honour me with your presence for dinner, take the carriage I will send to your rooms at eight o'clock tonight.'

Adrian waited for more, but no words came. 'It is not signed?'

'Nor is there a salutation.'

'Give it here. I wish to examine it.' He set his breakfast aside and took the paper, running his fingers over it, wishing that he could feel the meaning in the words. There was no indication that they would be dining alone, but neither was there a sign that others would be present.

'And there is no clue as to the identity of the sender? No address? A mark of some sort?' Although he'd have felt a seal or an embossed monogram with his own fingers.

'No, sir. I assumed you knew the identity of the woman.'

Adrian raised the paper to his nose. There was the slightly acrid smell of fresh ink, and a hint of lemon perfume. Had she rubbed the paper against her body, or merely touched it to the perfume bottle to send this part of the message?

He smiled. And did she know how she would make him wonder on the fact? He preferred to think of the paper held against those soft breasts, close to her quickly beating heart.

'About that…' What a blatant display of poor character that he had not even learned her name. It gave him no comfort to show Hendricks how low he had sunk, for the man was more than just a servant to him, after years together in the army, and Adrian's growing dependence on him since the injury. But as Hendricks's devotion to Lady Folbroke had grown, Adrian had come to suspect that the man's loyalties were more than usually torn.

'There was no time for a formal introduction last night. I had only just met her a few moments before you arrived. And, as I'm sure you could see, the situation was quite hectic.' He paused for a moment to let his secretary make what he could of that, and then said, 'But you saw her, did you not? What was she like?'

He heard Hendricks shift uneasily again. He had never before required the poor man to help with a liaison. It must prick at his scruples to be forced to betray the countess. But Adrian's curiosity about the woman would not be denied. 'Was she attractive?' he suggested.

'Very,' admitted Hendricks.

'Describe her.'

'Dark blond hair, short and dressed in curls. Grey eyes, a determined chin.'

Determined. He could believe that about her. Last night, she'd shown fortitude and a direct way of speaking that proved she was not easily impressed by fine words. He could feel the attraction for her, crackling on his skin like the air before a storm. 'And?' he prompted, eager to know more.

'She was expensively dressed.'

'And when you returned her to her home, where was it? It was you that escorted her, was it not?'

Hendricks shifted again. 'She made me swear, on my honour, not to give further information about her identity or her direction. You have a claim upon my honesty, of course. You are my employer…'

Adrian sighed. 'But I would not use that claim to make you break your word to a lady.'

'Thank you, my lord.'

'And I expect she will divulge what she wishes me to know, if I go to her tonight.'

He heard another uncomfortable shifting.

'And I will not expect you to be further involved in this, Hendricks, other than to help me with the reading of any correspondence. I understand that you are a valuable aid to Emily, as well as myself. I will not force you into a position more difficult than the one you already occupy.'

'Thank you, my lord.'

'This evening, I will take the carriage when it arrives, and whatever thanks the woman wishes to give me. I suspect that will be the end of it. You will hear no more of it.'

'Very good, my lord.' But Hendricks's voice sounded annoyingly doubtful.

Chapter Seven

At a tap on his shoulder, Adrian lifted his chin to make it easier for the valet to shave him for the second time that day. He did not like the feelings of helplessness that the process of dressing raised in him. They were ridiculous, of course. He had stood for it his entire life. And it was done just the same as it had been, when his eyes had been good. But now that he could not see to do it himself, he sometimes had the childish urge to slap the helping hands away.

He focused on the letter in his hand to calm his nerves. When the mysterious woman in the tavern had refused him, it was because of what she could see, and not what he could. She had thought him slovenly and commented on his drunkenness. It had made him regret the numbing effects of gin for the first time in ages. She was right, of course. If he valued her company, he would need a clear head to appreciate it, just as she wished for a lucid partner.

To show his respect on their second meeting, he must be immaculate. It was not a condition he was likely to achieve by himself, and he should be grateful for what his servant could do. He rubbed a hand along his own finished jaw. Perfectly smooth. He stood to accept the shirt, the cravat and the coat, and the final brushing of hair and garments, before his man announced him finished.

Then he walked the three paces to the doorway, stopped and turned back, setting the letter aside and picking up the miniature of Emily to drop it in its usual place in his coat pocket. It would serve as a reminder, should the attractiveness of his companion make him forget where his true heart and duty were promised. Tonight would be an enjoyable evening. But nothing more than that.

He travelled out of his room, took the ten paces through the sitting room, through the front door, and down the four steps to the street.

He could hear the carriage waiting in front of him, smell leather and horses, and see the dim shape of it, clearer at the edges, but fading to impenetrable blackness at the centre. The touches of vision that still remained were almost more maddening than nothing would be, for it gave the futile hope that the picture might suddenly clear if he blinked, or that a slight turn of the head and shift of the eyes would make it easier to see what lay in the fringes.

He calmed himself. It was only when he did not chase clarity that he could use what sight he had. A groom stepped forwards to help him, and this time he shook off the assistance, feeling along the open door in front of him to find the strap, searching with his toe for the step that had been placed, and then up and into the seat. The man closed the door and signalled to the driver, and they were off.

To pass the time he counted turns, imagining the map of the city. Not too far from his own home. This would put him in Piccadilly. And then, past. They travelled for a short time more, and then the carriage stopped, the door opened, and he could hear the step being put down for him again. The same groom that had been ready to help him up offered no hand this time, but murmured, 'A little to your left, my lord. Very good', allowing him to navigate on his own. When he had gained the street, the man said, 'The door you want is straight in front of you. Two scant paces. Then five stairs with a railing on your right. The knocker is a ring, set in a lion's mouth.'

'Thank you.' He must remember to compliment his hostess on the astuteness of her servants. With a few simple actions, this man had relieved the trepidation Adrian often felt in strange surroundings. Following the directions, he made his way to the door and knocked upon it.

It appeared the footman was prepared as well, describing the passage as they walked down it, opening the door to the sitting room and informing him of the locations of the furniture so that he did not have to fumble his way to the couch. He could feel the fire in front of him, but before he sat down he paused. The air smelled of lemons. Did her scent linger in the room? No. He could hear her breathing, if he listened for it. He turned in the direction of the sound. 'Did you mean to trick me into rudeness? You are standing in the corner, aren't you?'

She gave a small laugh and he enjoyed the prettiness of the sound. 'I did not think it necessary to have a butler announce you. We are meeting in secret, are we not?'

He walked towards her, praying that the confidence of the movement would not be spoiled by unseen furniture. 'If you wish it.'

'I think I would prefer it that way, Adrian.'

He started, and then laughed at his own foolishness. 'I gave you my first name last night, didn't I? And got nothing in return for it, as I remember. Perhaps a full introduction on my part will encourage you to reveal more.'

'That is not necessary, Lord Folbroke,' she said. 'Even without your telling me, I recognised you last night. And you would recognise me, should you still have your sight.'

'Would I, now?' He paused to rack his brains, trying to place the sound of that voice with a name, or at least a face. But when none appeared, he shrugged apologetically. 'I am embarrassed to admit that I do not know you, even now. And I hope you do not mean to punish me by keeping the secret.'

'I am afraid I must. Should I give you any clue to

my identity, you would know me immediately. And this evening will end quite differently than I wish it to.'

'And how do you wish it to end?' he coaxed.

'In my bed.'

'Really?' He had not expected her to be so very blunt about a thing that they both knew to be true. 'And if you were to tell me your name?'

'Then it would be a significant stumbling block to that. It might give you reason to be angry with me, or to discover a distaste or a hesitance that you do not have now. It would change everything.'

So she was likely the wife of some friend of his. And she thought him honourable enough not to cuckold a chum. 'Perhaps that is true.' Or perhaps it wasn't. His character did not bear close scrutiny at this time.

She sighed. 'I would much prefer to have you think me a stranger, and to kiss me as you did last night, as though you had no thought for anything but the moment, and for me. As though you enjoyed it.'

'I did enjoy it,' he said. 'And apparently so did you if you are willing to go to such great lengths to do it again.'

'It was very nice,' she said politely. 'And unlike anything I have previously experienced.'

Should he discover that she was the wife of an old friend, he might be unwilling to continue. But he would have to hunt the man down and give him a lecture on the care and tending of his lady. Considering the state of his own marriage, the idea that he would give advice to anyone was laughable.

'It pains me to hear you say such. There was nothing

so unusual in the way I kissed you. You have been sorely neglected. And I would be honoured to rectify such a grievous error, if you will allow me to. Lips as sweet as yours are made to be kissed hard and often.'

She gave a loud sigh that ended in a little squeak of annoyance, as though she had thought herself too sensible to be swayed by his words. 'Not quite yet, I think. We should eat. Dinner has been laid for us in the next room and I would not wish it to get cold.'

'Allow me.' He took her hand in the crook of his arm, wondering what he was meant to do next. Pride was all well and good, but what did it save him, if he did not know where to lead her?

She sensed his dilemma. 'The door is in front of you. And a little to the right.'

'Thank you.' He walked forwards, and she let him guide him. He half wished that they'd cross the threshold and find themselves in a bedroom. Then he could rid himself of the tension that was building in him. But, no. He could smell a meal somewhere nearby. She showed no hesitation, so he walked forwards into the blur in front of him, putting his hand out nonchalantly to feel for the table that he was sure must lay before them.

There it was. His fingers touched the corner and a linen cloth. He led her to what he hoped was an acceptable chair and worked his way to the other side, finding his seat and taking it and running his hand over the plate in front of him to familiarise himself with the setting.

Now the tension in him was of an entirely different sort. Suppose he spilled his wine, or dropped the meat into his lap without noticing? Suppose, dear God, she served him soup? If he made a fool of himself, he might never have the chance to know her better.

Adrian listened for the approach of the servant, and sniffed the food he was served. Was it fish? Or perhaps lamb. There was rosemary there, he was sure. And fresh peas, for there was the smell of mint. Problematic, for they would roll across the plate, if he was not careful. Better to flatten them with the fork than to chase them about the plate.

There was a faint laugh from the other side of the table, and his head snapped up. 'What is it?'

'You are glaring at your plate as though it is an enemy. And you seem to have forgotten me entirely. I am trying to decide whether to be amused or insulted by it.'

'I apologise. It is just that, meals can be a difficult time for me.'

'Do you require assistance?'

'That will not be necessary.' It humiliated him to display his weakness so clearly, and he longed to end the game they were playing and lie with her. Once their bodies touched, she could see how little this mattered.

But she had ignored him, for he could hear her drawing her chair closer to his. 'I said I did not need your help.' His tone was sharper than he had intended.

But it did not seem to bother her, for her response was placid enough. 'That is a pity. For it might be quite pleasant for both of us.'

He started as she touched his mouth with her finger,

resting the tip on the centre of his lower lip, almost as though it were a kiss.

He touched his tongue to it and tasted wine. She had dipped her finger into the glass.

He reached out, very carefully, to his own glass, dipping a finger in the contents, and then following the sound of her voice to try to touch her lip.

She laughed again, catching his hand and bringing it the last few inches to her mouth to kiss it clean. At the touch of her tongue, his own mouth went so dry he could hardly speak.

'You see?' she whispered. 'It might not be so bad to accept my help.'

'But I would not want to grow used to being hand fed, no matter how attractive the hands might be.'

She laughed. 'My hands might be ugly for all you know. And my face as well.'

He pulled his hand away from her lips, clasping her fingers in his. Then he turned it over, stroking the fingers, rubbing his thumb along the palm, over the back, circling the wrist. The fingers were long, the nails short, the skin soft. He held it to his cheek. 'The hand is lovely, as is the woman. You will never convince me otherwise.'

She sighed in response and he could feel her lean towards him as the pressure of her hand increased. 'You flatter, sir. But you do it well.'

'And you tempt. I am utterly captivated.' Which was not so much flattery as truth. He was hard for her, and they had not even begun to eat. But while he could not change his body's reaction, control of the evening was returning to him, and with it, he relaxed and focused on his ultimate goal. 'Before we go further, am I to be your only company tonight?'

'Of course.' She seemed surprised that he would ask. Surely that was a good sign.

'Then I take it that you still have not found your husband? Or have you found him, and are punishing him for leading you into last night's danger?'

She gave a little hiss of surprise and snatched her hand away. 'I did not betray my husband. It was he who left me. I have not seen him in some time. And I suspect he would make sport of my search for him, just as you do.'

'I am sorry. I did not mean to remind you of unhappiness. I only wished to ascertain that we would be alone for the whole evening.' To cover the awkward moment, he went back to his meal. As unobtrusively as possible, he touched the food on his plate to learn its location, then wiped his fingers on the napkin and reached for a knife to cut the chop he had found. He could hear the scrape of her cutlery as she began to eat as well.

Then she spoke. 'We need have no fear of interruption. This is not actually my home. It was let so that I might entertain in private. And tonight I am expecting no one else.'

So she had ample funds, and took scrupulous care of her reputation. He could not help trying to guess her identity from the clues she was giving him. 'Have you brought many admirers here?'

'There have been no others. Only you.'

His pulse quickened.

'Do not think that I have not had offers,' she added, as though she did not wish him to think her unworthy of masculine attention. 'But they know that I am married. And that I will not allow them to do the things they hint at when they are alone with me.'

'And yet you invited me here?' He smiled at her. 'I am truly flattered. What is the reason for my good fortune?'

'You are different.'

The way she said that word felt wonderful and strange, as though she thought it a good thing to be unlike one's fellows. Perhaps it was, if it attracted such a woman to him. 'I spend much of my time wishing I were not. But you seem to deem it an advantage.'

'I am not talking about your sight.'

'What then?'

'You are more handsome than the others, for one thing. And more brave.' Her voice still had the solid, matter-of-fact quality of the previous evening, but he could almost feel the warmth of her blush on his own skin.

'And what would make you think that?'

'The way you protected me last night. I doubt that the men who normally seek me out would have the courage to do that with two good eyes. But you did not think twice.'

'Which proves me a foolish drunkard, more than a hero.'

'I think it may be possible to be both.'

And he felt the little puff of pride, along with the

desire coursing in his blood. 'And you wish to reward me for my gallantry with dinner?'

'I told you before that it was more than that. I invited you here because you seemed to desire me. But I was not sure, when you were sober, that you would wish to come. I thought it would be better, should I be wrong, to enjoy a nice meal, than to sit alone, *en deshabille,* waiting for a man who did not want me.' The need in her voice was evident, though she'd tried to disguise it with a light tone. Without thinking, Adrian reached out for her, almost knocking over his water goblet in the process. She steadied it effortlessly, meeting his hand with hers on the stem of the glass.

'I think I have had quite enough to eat,' he said, guiding the glass to his lips for a sip of water before kissing the fingers that rested beside his on the goblet. 'If I had known that you were dressed to seduce me when I entered, I doubt we would have made it as far as the table.' He put down the glass again and stood. Then he took a step closer to her, listening to see if she moved away.

There was a faint hitch in her breathing as she rose. 'I had not expected it to be so easy to trap you. Should I take it as a compliment? Or is it that you are none too particular about your conquests?'

Was that bitterness he heard? 'Are you angry with me for coming when summoned?'

'Perhaps I am angry at myself for doing the summoning.' There was another pause. 'Or perhaps, now that the moment grows close, I cannot maintain a facade of sophistication. While I might wish to pretend otherwise, to be with you like this frightens me.'

There was that hint of vulnerability in her voice again, and it drew him to her in a way that was very different than the simple lust of the night before. He closed the distance between them and put his arms around her body, feeling her stiffen, and then relax. 'Do not feel the need to play the coquette to hold my interest. Or to continue with the act, should you change your mind. I wish to know you just as you are. And I wish to give you pleasure.' And for a moment, he took comfort at how good it felt to have something to offer her, and to know that the night might be about more than his needs.

'Of course,' she said. 'The bedchamber is on the other side of the sitting room. If you wish to retire there, I do not mind…' Her body tensed again.

'There is no need to rush,' he assured her, stroking her shoulder. 'You were quite right to think that I desired you. I have been on tenterhooks the whole day, fearing that I misunderstood your offer. And if I seemed to rush through my meal, it was not because I wanted to be elsewhere. I worried that I would do something laughable, or give you a distaste of me.'

'By dining with me?' she said. 'What a strange notion. I would never find you laughable, unless you sought to amuse me. And I'm sure that when you upset me, it will have little to do with your table manners.'

'When I upset you? You seem most sure of the fact, madam.'

'Of course. You will have your way with me—and then be off. That is your intention, is it not?'

And what could he say to that? For that had been his intention exactly.

'But I am hoping that, after all of your bragging last night, that the experience is sufficient to assuage some of the pain of your departure.'

What had her bastard of a husband done to her that she was so eager to be used, and yet so convinced that she could not hold his interest for more than a night? It put him in mind to prove her wrong. 'But suppose that was not my intention at all?'

She seemed to shrink, as though she wished to evaporate, even as he held her close. Then she said softly, with none of the confidence he'd grown used to, 'Have I done something wrong?'

'On the contrary. You are more right than I ever imagined. Why do you ask?'

'If you do not want me...'

'Of course I want you, my darling. But things have more flavour if we take the time to savour them. Is there a couch by the fire where we might take our wine and sit for a time?' He could feel her taking a breath, ready to object. So he reached carefully and found the tip of her nose with his finger. 'Do not worry. When the time is right, I mean to take you to bed.' From there, he touched her chin with the same finger, guiding himself to her face until her lips met his. The briefest kiss was a taste of heaven, just as it had been the previous night. 'As a matter of fact, I doubt I will be able to help myself.'

He kissed her again, slowly. Her mouth tasted of wine. He ran his knuckles over the curve of her shoulder, and felt the smooth fabric of her clothing. 'What are you wearing? I think it is a dark colour. And it feels like silk. But beyond that…'

'It is but a robe. Blue silk.'

'Describe the colour. Is it like the sea? A robin's egg?'

She thought for a moment. 'I think it could be called sapphire.'

'And what do you wear under it?'

He heard her swallow nervously. 'My nightdress.'

Adrian wrapped his arms more tightly about her, stroking her body lightly, so as to satisfy his curiosity without arousing her. He felt no stays or petticoats. And he damned his eyes for their betrayal. He would not have been able to take food had he known that on the other side of the table there had been only a few layers of fabric between him and the softness of this woman's body.

She was straining on tiptoe to match his height, kissing his ear with little licks of her tongue. He could feel each touch of it to the soles of his feet. 'Let us sit,' he whispered again. 'Show me where to go.'

She slipped out of his arms and took him by the hand to lead him into the fog of the room, through a doorway, towards the glow of a fire. She sat him down on the grey blob before it, which turned out to be some kind of sofa, and he pushed her gently back against the arm of it. 'Before I kiss you again, I would like to touch you.' He wondered if it sounded strange to her. But there was so much he still did not know about her. It would not have mattered what she looked like if his intent had been to leave before the dawn. But with this woman? Somehow everything was different.

He could feel the hesitation as she tried to decipher the request. And then she said, 'Where?'

He laughed. 'Everywhere. But let us begin at the beginning, shall we?' He reached out a tentative finger to touch her hair.

Curls, just as Hendricks had said. Although he'd thought he enjoyed long hair on a woman, the texture was interesting. He could feel the carefully styled ringlets at the side, the pins that held them in place, and the way they revealed the smoothness of her neck. He dipped his head close and found the place at its base where scent had been dabbed, inhaling deeply and touching the point with his tongue.

She gave a little jump of surprise.

He ran his fingers along the place his lips had touched, finding the tendons, the hollows, feeling movement as she swallowed. It was a lovely, long neck and he wondered if the complexion was pale or a dusky gold.

Her chin was well shaped, with a firmness that hinted at stubbornness. She'd proven that already, so it was no real surprise. And there was her mouth. He smiled, remembering the taste of it. High cheekbones, a dimple, a raised brow. He smoothed it, feeling the tiny wrinkle of confusion on the forehead and the beat of a pulse in her temple. Her eyes were closed. He brushed them with his thumb, feeling the long lashes lying upon her cheeks. When they were open, he was sure that the look in those eyes would be probing, discerning, intelligent. But she would look like a child when she slept, gentled and at peace.

'Did you discover what you wished to know?' He heard another faint twinge of doubt in her voice, as though she feared that she had been found wanting on close inspection.

'You are beautiful. Just as I knew you would be.'

He could feel the heat in her cheeks, the little puff of exhaled breath, and the way her body relaxed beside his, knowing he approved of her.

Then he cupped his hand at the back of her neck, and brought her lips to his to take them as they opened to speak. Her tongue touched his eagerly, and she put her hands on his shoulders, holding him in place as though she suspected, at any moment, that he would regain his senses and reject her.

He took her mouth with deep greedy strokes of his tongue, letting his hands roam lightly over her body, feeling the heat of her through the fabric. Then he found the tie of her robe and reached beneath it, tugging her nightdress upwards until he caught the hem, pulling it until it rested even with her nipples and left her lower body sheathed in nothing but smooth blue silk. He stroked her side through the robe, moving the fabric against her until she gasped with pleasure and fought to free herself from her clothing.

He laughed, rubbing the rougher cloth of the dress against her nipples, dipping his mouth to the bare undersides of the exposed slopes beneath it, kissing the peachskin softness of them, licking up to the place where they puckered with excitement.

Her struggling ceased and she went still, waiting for the moment when he would uncover her. When he did not move, she arched her back and moaned, and he pulled the fabric aside suddenly and feasted upon her, drawing them in turn into his mouth, sucking hard, squeezing them with his hand.

'Adrian.' Her voice was tortured, desperate. 'Adrian, finish quickly.'

'I am just beginning, my love.'

'But I fear… I think I am ill…I feel so strange…' The words came out in a series of gasps.

And he wondered—could it be that a married woman might still be a virgin to her own pleasure? He released her breasts, slowing his attack to let her calm. 'You will be fine, darling. But you must trust me to know what is best for you. Now help me remove your gown.' He kissed her on the mouth again as he reached to untie the belt. She struggled out of the sleeves, and between them they pushed the cotton nightrail over her head and to the floor.

'Now lie back upon the silk. Relax. There is a place on your body as wondrous as the pearl in an oyster. And I mean to touch you there until you submit to me.' He sank his fingers into the warmth between her legs, deeper between the folds of her to find the spot that he knew would drive her mad. With his other hand, he found the belt of the robe and its silk tasseled ends, drawing one up her belly to dangle it back and forth over her breasts.

She was sobbing now, shaking as though she would fight against the release. So he slowed his hand, resting the pad of his thumb against her as he let his fingers sink deep inside her. She was hot, tight and wet, and he would go there himself soon. And as he stroked he felt an answering throb in his loins to match the one against his hand as her body gave up the last of her control to him.

'Adrian,' she cried louder than his pounding heartbeat, 'I am yours.' He could feel her, collapsed on her back before him, legs spread wide around his hand, ready to be taken.

He had thought to take her to bed, to carry her if he could. But it was quite impossible, for he could not stand to wait. He curled his fingers inside her and made her shudder again as he fumbled with the buttons on his trousers, and then in his pocket for the sheath he carried.

She froze, and then he felt her scrambling, crablike, away from his touch. 'What is that?'

He reached for her again. 'I do not expect you have ever seen such a thing. It is called a French letter.'

'And what is its intended purpose?' she asked.

He wanted to groan to her that there was no time for questions, and to put the thing on and ram himself home. But he struggled through the roar of desire in his head to be patient for the sake of her innocence. 'One might call it a preventative. It can be worn by the man during the physical act of love.'

'And just what do you seek to prevent?' she said, distant and cold.

He gritted his teeth to keep his temper and lust in check. 'Several things. Disease, for example.'

'You think I have an illness?' She struggled off the sofa and he heard a wine glass clink against the side table before tumbling to the carpet.

'Of course not. You are a lady, and have limited experience with such things. But by my recent behaviour, I can hardly be called a gentleman. And it is better, if one cannot see, to be more careful than usual, when one decides to…' He let the sentence hang open.

'I found you yesterday, dead drunk in a gin mill, brawling with navvies. And now you wish me to believe that you care so much for your own health, and the health of your women, that you would bother with such a thing?' The innocence was gone now, replaced by the tart, demanding tone that he had heard yesterday.

'Better a quick death in a fight than a slow death of the pox.' He patted his knee, inviting her back on to his lap.

'Get out,' she muttered, stepping even farther away.

'Does it really bother you so?' He stuffed the thing back in his pocket, wondering if it were possible to make her forget it again.

'Perhaps it bothers me to think of you consorting with who knows whom. And then coming to me, treating me as a nothing, just as you have always done. Leave me immediately,' she said more loudly.

'Darling…' he gave a diminishing laugh, as though it would be so easy to reduce the pain of what she was doing to him by her delay '…it is for the best, really.

You are married, and so am I. We do not wish to risk an accident of another sort. Suppose you were to get with child?'

'Of course we would not want that.' Her voice was well on the way to being shrewish now. 'Why would anyone wish to get a child on me? It is good that you cannot see, I am sure, for you would find me so repellent that you would run from me, after only a few days.'

'That is not it at all,' he muttered, his desire for her dying in annoyance with her foolish need for reassurance. 'I am sure that you are most beautiful, as I have already said.'

'Liar,' she said, and the word ended in a sob. 'Liar. Get out. Go away. Do not touch me.' She pulled the silk robe around her body with a swish to make sure that he heard.

'You were quite willing enough to have me touch you a few minutes ago. I do not understand your sudden change of heart.'

'Well, I understand quite enough for both of us. You refuse to lie with me in a normal manner. And so I refuse to lie with you at all.' She stomped her foot hard enough for him to feel the vibrations of the floor through his boot soles. 'Get out.'

He stood, doing up his buttons, wanting to storm out the door and to the street, to take the first carriage he could find far away from this place, so that he would never have to see her again.

And then he barked his shin on the little table beside the couch, and remembered that he could not see her at all. Nor could he remember the way to the door. He was wilting with shame now, red faced, limp and weak and helpless in the presence of a woman he desired. 'I am sorry. But I will not...I cannot...'

'Of course you could. If you thought, even for a moment, about what damage you have done to those who care for you...'

'No. It is not that at all.' What she was saying made no sense, and had nothing to do with the confusion he was suffering. 'Believe me, at this moment, I want nothing more than to leave this place and forget this evening as soon as I am able.'

Then he held his hand out in resignation. 'But I will need someone to give me my stick and find my coat and hat, for I cannot. Then you will need to call a servant to lead me to a carriage, unless you mean to turn me helpless into the street. Or maybe you wish to laugh at my struggles.' A thought occurred to him. 'Perhaps that was your game all along. Does it amuse you to see me in such a state over you, and then reject me, knowing how easy it will be to escape?'

'Of course,' she bit back. 'Because everything that happens is about you and your pride and what people will think. For a few moments tonight, I was foolish enough to think that you were not the most selfish man in the world.' She pushed him on the shoulder to spin his body a quarter-turn. 'The door is in front of you. Straight forwards. Go.'

She did not say another word to him, but walked at his side until he was in the entrance hall. Was she ashamed at her outburst, or as disgusted by his weakness as he was? In either case, he knew she did not want him enough to relent, for she went to the bell to ring for aid.

As they waited in silence for a servant to come and lead him out, he felt carefully over buttons, arranging his clothes as best he could, double and triple checking to be sure he had not done up his trousers crooked, so that it was not obvious to all that he had left in haste from an assignation. When he was sure he would not shame himself further, he said, 'And now you know why I am so careful not to spread my seed. This curse that has rendered me helpless came to me because my father, and his before him, had no compunctions about breeding. I have no intention of making the same mistake, leaving my son a useless joke of a man. It is the reason I fled my own marriage. And it is why I will not join unhindered with you. I am sorry if that displeases you, but it is a fact of life, and cannot be changed. Good evening to you, madam.'

Chapter Eight

Emily waited until she was sure that her husband was well on his way before moving from the doorway. As it was, she hoped he had not known that she watched him climb into the carriage to make sure he got to it safely. He was not a child. He did not need her help. And it would hurt him even more if she showed a final lack of confidence.

There was some relief in knowing that she had had her trunks moved to the bedroom of this apartment. At least she would not be forced to creep back to the Eston town house and risk revealing to her brother David the depths of her foolishness.

But she felt she must share some small part of the truth with someone if she was to keep from going mad. So she signalled the footman who had just helped Adrian out the door that she wished to speak with Mr Hendricks, and to go with haste to the rooms to retrieve him, before Lord Folbroke had returned to them.

Then she went to her bedchamber and summoned her maid, requesting that all evidence of her tryst with Adrian be removed from the sitting room and that she be dressed in a way more appropriate for a visitor.

But a part of her, newly awake and alive, did not want to dress. It wanted to recline upon the bed and revel in the touch of silk on skin, and the memory of her husband's hands on her body.

This had been both the best and the worst night of her life. For most of it, he had been everything she had imagined he could be. Gentle one moment, forceful the next. But ever aware of her needs, eager to please her before he took pleasure.

And the pleasure he had given… She hugged her arms close to her body, feeling the silk shift over her aching breasts. Lord have mercy upon her, she still wanted him. Her skin was hot from his touches, and her body cried out that she had been a fool to let pride stand in the way of a more complete union between them.

Until he had produced his little sheath, she had all but forgotten how his neglect had hurt her, or how far she was from forgiving him. She had not thought further than the immediate need for intimate contact with his body, unhindered passion, and for even the smallest possibility that she might bear his child.

That was what she had come here for, after all. And once the idea had planted itself in her mind, it had grown there, not unlike the baby she was seeking. If she could not have Adrian, then perhaps she could have some small part of him to raise and to love.

But now it appeared that this had been the precise reason he had left her. In his present state of mind, even if he went back to Derbyshire for a time to appease his cousin, he would refuse to touch her. He would die recklessly as his father had and leave her alone, just as she feared.

Even pretending that she was not his wife—it had not been as she had expected. She'd imagined the separation to be a personal thing. He was avoiding her in particular, but giving himself with abandon, body and soul, to any other woman that struck his fancy. In anonymity, she might have some share in what others had received from him. But it seemed the act was only a gratification of a physical urge, and that there had never been trust from his side at all. He kept himself apart both from her and any other woman he might lie with.

A footman tapped upon her door to signal that Hendricks awaited her in the sitting room. Her maid, Hannah, gave a final tug upon the sash to her dress and pronounced her respectable, and she went to greet the secretary. But entering the sitting room brought on a flood of embarrassing memories and she hurried to take a seat upon the couch before the fire, gesturing him to a chair opposite.

'My lady?' From the way he looked at her, she wondered if some clue remained in the room or about her person that might indicate what had gone little more than an hour before. He watched her too closely as she entered, lingering on her dress, her body and her face in a way that was most inappropriate.

'You wish to know what occurred, I suppose?' she said, trying not to let her failure be too obvious.

'Of course not.' The poor man must have realised that he had been staring. He looked away quickly and then went quite pink, probably afraid that he had been dragged out of bed to receive some all-too-personal revelation on her part.

'You have nothing to fear.' Emily scowled back at him. 'The evening was without incident.'

'Without…' He looked back at her and pushed his spectacles up the bridge of his nose as he sometimes did when surprised. But behind the lenses, his eyes narrowed as though he doubted her word.

'Well, very nearly,' she said, trying to find an appropriate way to explain. 'The situation is much more complicated than I feared. When I came to London, I had assumed for years that Adrian had a distaste of me, and that that was why he abandoned me in the country. Since I knew he did not like me, I thought there was little future for us, beyond the arrangement we have come to. One cannot change one's nature, after all.

'But our estrangement is not about me at all. He avoids me because he actively seeks to die without issue. He thinks by doing so, and letting Rupert take the title, that he can stamp out the weakness in his family…which is utter nonsense. But it means that I am the last woman in the world he wishes to know.'

'But his idea is not without merit,' Hendricks said

sensibly. 'It is logical that he would want a healthy heir, and to believe that his own child might share his problems.'

She glared at him. 'I do not care to hear about the logic. I am sure, if we get out the family history and examine it, we will see some of the earls from this very line lived long and successful lives, fully sighted to their last day. As have many of the second sons and daughters. And it is quite possible, if we examine Rupert's branch of the family, that we will find similar problems with blindness there. His own father was nearly sightless upon death, was he not?'

Hendricks nodded. 'But nothing was made of it, because he was not Folbroke.'

'Then Adrian's plans are quite—Lord forgive me the expression—short sighted. It is only a medical anomaly that has caused the weakness in the last three earls, and not some dire curse upon the heir to Folbroke.'

'The line would need new blood entirely to solve the problem,' Hendricks admitted.

'How democratic,' she said drily. 'Next you will suggest that I be bred like a mare to someone healthy, for the good of the succession.' She shuddered in revulsion. 'I believe I should have some choice in the matter. And like it or not, I choose the husband I already have. Perhaps Adrian thinks our marriage was forced upon him. But from the first moment I can remember, I have wanted no other man, nor is that likely to change now that I have seen his situation.' She sat up straight and reached into a pocket for a handkerchief to wipe away the mote that was making her eyes tear. 'We do not always want the person who is best for us, I am afraid.'

'The poets never claim that the path of true love is an easy one,' Hendricks added in a dejected tone.

'No poetry was necessary to prove that for myself tonight.'

'Then you told him who you were?'

'I most certainly did not,' she said, and was annoyed to notice the hole in her own logic. Her current under-standing of her husband did not negate her previous one. While he had been most attentive to her when he thought her a stranger, he had not mentioned his feelings for his wife at all. 'Things were difficult enough, without bring-ing my identity into the conversation. If he'd known I was his wife, we'd have...' she shrugged, embarrassed '...we'd have got much less close to the thing he was avoiding than we already have.'

Hendricks was looking at her with a kind of horri-fied curiosity. She had spoken too much, she was sure. With a hurried wave of her hand, as though she could wipe the words from the air, she said, 'I am sure, if I'd told him who I was, he'd have been quite angry at being tricked. It would be better, I think, to wait until I can find some other way to explain. And a time when he is in an exceptionally good mood.' And let Hendricks wonder as much as he liked what might cause an improvement in her husband's disposition.

She went on. 'But tonight, he left angry. And it was my fault. We argued over...something. And when I turned him out, I had forgotten that he could not see to find his own way to the door. To see him standing there, proud, and yet helpless?' And now, when she raised her handkerchief, she could not deny that it was to wipe away a tear. 'He needs me.'

'That he does, my lady.' Hendricks seemed to relax in his seat, like a man who had found a patch of solid ground after getting lost in a bog.

'I need you to deliver another letter to him, similar to the one you did this morning. Lord knows if he will welcome it, for I am sure he is very cross after the way I behaved tonight. But I mean to try again, tomorrow night, to gain his trust.'

When Adrian awoke the next morning, the lack of headache made the feelings of regret more sharp. He had come back to his rooms, ready to rave at Hendricks about the vagaries of the female mind. But the man, who seemed to have no life at all outside of his work, had chosen that evening to be away from the house.

And then he'd thought to find a bottle and a more sensible woman. Liquor would lift his spirits and a whore would not refuse the predilections of any man with the money to buy her time. In fact, the ladies of that profession were often somewhat relieved that a client would take the time to protect himself.

But a gentlewoman would have no such understanding. To her it was a grave insult to even mention such a thing. To imply that she was not clean enough, and to do it to a woman that had already felt the sting of rejection?

Any frustration that he felt after tonight was his own

fault. And his own discomfort was probably a deserved punishment for leading the woman to believe he was worthy of her, and then leaving her disappointed and insulted. In the end, he had called for a single glass of brandy and taken it with him to his own large and empty bed.

This morning, the rattle of the curtains came as usual, but the daylight following it seemed more of a gradual glow than a rush of fire. 'Hendricks.'

'Yes, my lord.'

'It is still morning, is it not?'

'Half past ten. You retired early.'

'Earlier than you, it seems.'

'Yes, my lord.' His secretary showed no interest in sharing his activities of the previous evening, and Adrian regretted the loss of the easy camaraderie they'd shared while fighting together in Portugal. At one time, they'd have gone out together, or shared the stories of their exploits over breakfast the next morning.

'Lady Folbroke required my services.'

And that was the true reason for the breach, more than their inequality of rank, or his growing helplessness. And for a moment, Adrian wondered if there was a reason for the timing of the visit. When better to go to her, than when one could be sure that her husband would be occupied elsewhere? 'She is well, I trust.'

'When I left her, yes.'

Did that imply that she was the better for Hendricks's company? They would make a handsome couple, similar in colouring and disposition, taciturn but intelligent.

And yet the idea disturbed him, and he rushed to replace the image of them together that formed in his mind. 'I congratulate you on your success. Would that my own evening had gone as well. It seems I am no longer fit company for a lady, for I could not manage a few hours in the presence of one without offering insult.'

Hendricks requested no details, nor did he offer to correct any misconceptions about his own activities. Adrian heard the nervous rattling of the morning paper against the post. 'Do you wish me to read the news, my lord? Or shall I begin with the mail?'

'The mail, I think.' If he did not intend to attend Parliament when it was in session, then hearing the news of the day only made him feel helpless.

'There is only one letter here. And it is similar to the one you received yesterday.'

'Similar in what way?' He doubted it would be in content, after the way they had parted.

'In handwriting, and lack of a return direction. The wax is the same, but unmarked. I have not opened it.' Hendricks gave a delicate pause. 'I thought it better to wait upon your instructions.'

The embarrassment from last evening was still fresh, and a part of him wanted to throw the missive in the fire, unread. What would she have sent, so soon after parting from him? An angry diatribe? A curt dismissal? Florid words of love or a description of their activities on the couch were unlikely. But they would be particularly awkward today, delivered in Hendricks's pleasant baritone as Adrian tried not to imagine the man doing similar things with his Emily.

He steeled his nerves and said, as casually as possible, 'Best read it, I suppose, for the sake of curiosity if nothing else.'

There was a crackling of paper as the wax seal was released, and Hendricks unfolded the note.

'I am sorry. If you would accept this apology, return tonight.'

So even after last night, she still wanted to see him. He felt both relief and shame that she should think she was the one who needed to apologise—and damned lucky that he would have a chance to set her straight.

But was it worth the risk of another rejection? If she meant to toy with him, then so be it. Even after the disasters of the previous two nights, he felt a singing in his blood at the thought that he might kiss her again, and that she might let him take more liberties than he had as yet achieved.

He grinned up at his secretary, who said benignly, 'Will there be a reply?'

The things he wished to say to her came and passed in a rush, as he realised that they would need to be filtered through poor Hendricks, who would be feeling as uncomfortable as he. He had never before forced the man into a position of writing a billet-doux, nor would he today. 'Normally, I would wish to send something immediately. But she has given no address. And after several hours in her company, I still have no idea what to call her, for she would not even give me her first name. If she wishes to shroud herself in mystery, I have no objection. But for punishment, she may wait in ignorance of my feelings until I see her tonight.'

Chapter Nine

Emily paced the front hall of the rented flat, unable to contain her agitation at the thought of the evening's meeting. She had waited nervously for some response from her husband. In the afternoon there had come a hurried note, directly from Hendricks, that she could expect a visit that evening. But there had been no mention of Adrian's reaction, whether he was angry, elated or indifferent.

She was both relieved and annoyed by this. While it was flattering to think that her rejection had not dampened his interest, she could not manage to forget that her husband thought he was rushing to a stranger with the intention of betraying his wife.

But then she remembered the feelings she had experienced on the previous evening. The things he had done to her were so different than his behaviour during the first week of their marriage that she could hardly believe he was the same person. If a revelation of her identity meant that they would be returning to the country for a life of such sterile conjugation, she much preferred being the mysterious object of his infidelity.

Promptly at eight, there was a knock on the door. Before the servant could arrive, she had opened it herself, and pulled Adrian into the hall with her.

At first he resisted, unwilling to be helped. But then he recognised her touch and submitted to her, fumbling to help with the closing of the door once he was through.

Before she could speak, he had seized her, the cane in his left hand bracing vertically along her spine as he kissed her. It was long and hard and unyielding, holding her body against his as he reached between them to unbutton his top coat with his right hand. With the open coat shielding them from observation, he began a careful examination of her dress with his fingers. 'A dinner gown tonight, my dear? Afraid to risk the nightdress again, I see. But what is this, here amongst the net and beads?' His hand cupped her breast. 'You have not bothered with stays. That is a welcome thing to a sightless man. I can read your response to my arrival with a touch.'

'You are terribly forward,' she said, but made no effort to remove his hand from her body as it brushed against her sensitive nipple.

'I am,' he admitted. 'And I had meant this evening to put you at your ease with my good manners. Already, I have failed.'

'It does not matter. I am happy that you returned. And for last night, I am sorry.'

His fingers left her breast and unerringly found her lips, and he laid one against them to stop the apology. 'It is I who must apologise. I was the one who offered insult. I treated you as I would treat someone who meant nothing to me.'

'Which is how it should be. You barely know me.'

'Now, perhaps. But I would like to know you better.' His head bowed to rest against hers, forehead to forehead. 'You could not understand my reasons for behaving as I did. And I gave you no reason to try. I thought only of my own needs, which were urgent, and offered no explanation for it.'

'It is all right. It does not matter.'

'It does. I hurt you. I made you feel that you are not worthy of love. But that is not the case.'

Emily laid a hand on the front of his vest, over his heart, and he clasped it there. They stood for a time, just like that, as though it had been ages since they had been together, and not hours. And for her, it had been. For how could a few evenings fill the void created by three years apart?

And as she thought of their marriage, she could feel the old breathlessness coming back, the terror of doing something wrong in his presence and spoiling this sudden intimacy. At last, she murmured into his lapel, 'Supper?'

Adrian groaned in frustration and tightened his arms upon her. 'Might it be possible to take light refreshment, and to sit before the fire? And I truly mean that we will talk tonight before anything else occurs between us. But you needn't keep me at arm's length across a table to ensure my good behaviour.'

It surprised her to find him as intimidated by a formal meal as she was in talking to him. 'Very well. I will have the servants lay something simple for us, if that is what you wish. Come.'

She led him to the couch, and arranged for a tray of cold meats and bread to be brought to them, along with wine and fruit. And then she sat down beside him, and offered him a grape. 'Do not think for a moment to deny me the pleasure of helping you.'

'If it means that you will sit close beside me and let me kiss the crumbs from your fingertips? Then of course.' He took the fruit from her hand, and said with a full mouth, 'And while I eat, you will tell me about your husband.'

'And…why would I do that?' She hurriedly offered him more food, wishing that there were a way to get him to the table again so that they could be equally uncomfortable.

He smiled back at her and wiped the corner of his mouth with a napkin. 'I will admit, there is an allure in an anonymous coupling. And a decided lack of guilt at parting from a stranger. But it has been a long time since I have been willing to play the fool for a woman. When I left here, I wanted to be angry, to blame you for all of it, and dismiss the incident from my mind. But I have brooded on it for most of last night and the better part of today as well. I want to know the meaning of your words.'

'What did I say that you did not understand?' She took a fortifying sip of wine.

'You seemed more offended that I feared to get you with child than you were with the implication that I might think you poxed. You may tell me that I have no right to enquire, but it makes me wonder at your motives in lying with me, and fear that you are seeking something other than pleasure. If you cannot give me a suitable explanation, than I must leave you.' He took her hand, and squeezed it. 'But I very much want to stay.'

Emily leaned back in her seat and took another sip of wine. It was as good a time as any to explain to him, she supposed. 'To make you understand, I must tell you about my marriage. My husband and I were together for but a brief time. And while we resided under the same roof, he barely spoke to me. As a matter of fact, he seemed to avoid my company.'

He gave a grunt of dismissal. 'I cannot believe it.'

'In his defence, I barely had the nerve to speak in his presence. I was quite in awe of him.'

'This surprises me,' he said. 'You seemed fearless when I first met you. You have a direct and intelligent manner of speaking that is most refreshing.'

'Thank you.' She coloured. For while the compliment was delivered unawares, it was welcome.

He traced a finger along her cheek. 'Of course, were I married to you, conversation would have been the last thing on my mind.'

'Oh, really. And what would be the first?'

'Getting you to bed, of course. Just as it was when I met you.'

'Then you are obviously not the man I married,' she said, 'for on the three times he visited my room—'

Adrian's brow furrowed. 'Three times?'

'Yes.'

He laughed. 'You mean in the first night, of course.'

She grimaced. He did not even recognise himself in the quite obvious clue she had given him. 'I mean in total. I remember it distinctly. How many women can, after several years of marriage, remember the exact number of conjugal visits and count them on less than a hand?'

'That is an abomination.'

'I quite agree.' And she hoped that the frosty tone in her voice might bring some mote of recollection from the man at her side.

'And these visits…' he cleared his throat as though to stifle a laugh '…were they in any way memorable?'

'I remember each instant, for they were my first and only experiences of that sort.'

'And how would you describe them?'

Her timidity forgotten, she finished her wine in a gulp and said, 'In a word? Disappointing.'

He seemed taken aback by this. 'Was he not gentle with you? Did he give no thought to your inexperience?'

'On the contrary. He proceeded with gentleness and all due care.'

'Then what was the problem?'

Emily almost growled in frustration, for it was clear that he had no memory at all of what had been the most important week of her life. 'He made it plain that he did not enjoy my company. My deflowering was done with martial efficiency, at a tempo that might have been more appropriate for a march than a frolic. And then he had returned to his rooms, without another word.'

Adrian gave a snort, before managing to master himself again. 'You know little of the army, if you think that men in the, uh, heat of battle…' And then, as though he remembered that he was speaking to a lady, he stopped. 'Well, then. Never mind. But you are right in thinking that such restraint could not have been pleasant for him. And did you tell him, the next day, of your dissatisfaction with his performance?'

'How could I? I was innocent of the subject. For all I knew, it was the same for all. I had been watching him for years, and dreaming of how it might be. And the waking truth was not at all as I expected. But when one can barely bring oneself to discuss the weather with the man to whom one is wed, how is one to explain that one had hoped, in the marriage bed, for something more?'

'I see.' He laid a hand on hers, in comfort.

'And the next night was the same. And then the next.' She was almost shaking with rage at the memory of it, and the returning shame. 'And then, it seemed he gave our marriage up as a bad job. When evening arrived, a servant informed me that he would be dining with friends, and that I was not to expect his company. And shortly thereafter, he removed to London and has not returned.'

His hand reached up to brush her cheek again, and she shied away, trying to hide the tears of shame that had come unbidden at the recitation.

'And all this time you thought it was somehow your fault?'

'What else could I think? And when you came to me, with that…thing? Is there something wrong with me, that a man I want does not wish to touch me as he should?'

Adrian laughed. 'It does no credit to my gender, but I assure you that there is little that a man cannot stomach when his appetite is good. I can find nothing about you so far that would lead me to believe you capable of inducing such a reaction. I might say, after last night's intimate inspection of you, that you are sweetly formed and temptation itself. You had reduced me to such a state when you turned me out that even with two good eyes I doubt I could have found the door.'

'Really?'

'If the man you married was sane and whole, he would have responded differently.'

'If he was whole,' she repeated.

Adrian nodded. 'Therefore, we must assume that the fault lies on his side. For myself, I would suspect impotence.'

She coughed on a bit of bread, and hurried to pour herself another glass of wine. 'Really?'

He nodded again. 'An inability to perform effectively, no matter how tempted. And he left before you might notice that he had given all he could. It is either that, or a penchant for other men.'

'Oh, I seriously doubt that,' she said, relieved that he could not see her smile.

'It is not unheard of, you know. When you find him in London, it is quite possible that you will discover his relationship with one of his friends is…unusually close.'

'I see.'

'But in either case, it has nothing to do with you, or your attractiveness to members of the opposite gender.'

'You think that is it?'

'I have no doubt. You married a fool, too ashamed to admit a flaw in his own person. And it has caused you grief.'

'When it is put to me thus, I think that is a very accurate assessment of the situation. Thank you for your opinion.' For, although she did not think him a fool, *per se,* the rest of the sentence was true enough.

But the Adrian that sat beside her now did not seem likely to repeat the mistakes he had made in the past. He took the glass from her hands and set it aside. Then he trailed his fingers along the skin of her arms, tracing the line of her shoulder and neck. It made her feel sleek, graceful, desired. 'Think of it no more.' He kissed her shoulder.

'Sometimes I find it hard to think of anything else,' she admitted. 'When I am alone at night.'

'And unsatisfied,' he whispered. 'It is a condition that is easily remedied. Allow me.'

'Allow you what?' She pulled away from him, somewhat surprised by the husky tone of his voice.

'Allow me to prove to you, as I did last night, that there is nothing wrong with you. And that the disappointment you experienced at the hands of your idiot husband need not be repeated.'

'Oh.' The word came out of her, part sigh and part moan, for his lips were on her throat, nuzzling at the place where her heart's blood beat. 'But last night, you said you could not lie with me without using that thing you brought. And I do not think I would like that at all.' For while she wished to have his baby, suddenly, she wished even more to feel her husband inside of her, unsheathed, and as besotted with her as he seemed tonight.

He paused his kisses and looked into her face, his eyes sightless, but still searching to reach her, to make her understand. 'If that one thing is so important to you, then I do not think it is possible for me to give you what you desire. There is only one woman on earth that could command such an intimacy from me. If I deny it of her and tell myself that it is done for her own good, but I give myself freely to another, I will sacrifice the last scrap of honour I have left.' Without thinking, he touched the pocket of his coat, in a place just over his heart.

'What were you reaching for, just now?' she asked.

'Nothing. It is foolishness, really. And certainly not the time…'

Emily ignored his protests, slipped her hand into his pocket and withdrew a battered miniature, no bigger than a locket. She'd remembered sitting for it when she was sixteen. She'd been quite miserable at the time, having just recovered from influenza.

'It is my wife, Emily,' he said softly.

Without thinking, she responded, 'It is not a very good likeness', forgetting that there was no way she could know. Then added, 'Those paintings never are.'

He smiled and took it back from her, opening the cover and running a thumb over the ivory that it was painted on. 'Perhaps not. But it hardly matters, for it has been some time since I've seen it clearly. Still, I like to look on it.' He held it in front of him as though pretending he could see it, then passed it to her.

The question of a likeness was no longer a matter. In the place he had touched it, he had rubbed the paint away from the ivory, smearing her eyes and leaving only a white smudge in the place where her lips might be.

'She was a sweet girl,' he said, smiling and reaching out to take it back. 'And from what I am told, she has grown into a fine woman.'

'You do not know?'

'It has been several years since I've seen her, and she has adjusted to my absence. She handles the business of the estate as well, if not better than I would. I sign what papers are needed when she sends them to me, of course. But her decisions are sound, and I have had no reason to question them. My holdings profit from her wisdom.'

'You treat her no better than your man of business, then?'

'Hardly,' he said. 'Our families were old friends, and

when we married, we had been betrothed for ages, promised to each other almost in the cradle. I had no problems with it, at first. But then I learned the fate of my father, and my grandfather before him.' He gave a wry shrug. 'It was clear that there could be no normal marriage between us. But it hardly seemed fair to her to cry off. I was by far the best offer the girl was likely to have.'

'Bloody cheek,' she murmured.

'But true, none the less. The title is an old one. The house and lands are enough to tempt any woman. By the time I wed her, she was nearly on the shelf. I had hoped that my neglect of her would put her off me. But she'd waited patiently for me to come back from the army when she could just as well have been at Almack's on the hunt for a better man.'

'Or you might have married her sooner,' she pointed out. 'Instead of risking your title by buying a commission.'

'True enough,' he agreed. 'The army is a better choice for a second son. It is dangerous for an heir to go into battle. My cousin Rupert was ecstatic, of course.' When she did not ask, he added, 'He is next in line for Folbroke.'

She responded with an 'I see' to hide her lack of ignorance on the subject. 'And are you pleased that he will succeed you? Is he worthy of it?'

Adrian frowned. 'He is my nearest male relative. It does not matter whether he is worthy or not.'

'Then you think he is not, or you would have answered in the affirmative without hesitation,' she said.

'He is not blind,' Adrian said, as though that answered all. 'And if desire for an earldom is an indicator of worthiness, then he has more worth than I possess. He wants the place more than I ever did. For my part, I expected Napoleon would finish me off before I had to admit the truth to Emily. Once gone, it would be no concern of mine. I would die gloriously and never have to face the future. Instead, a muzzle flash blinded me, and I was sent home. The surgeon told me that the damage to my eyes was a temporary thing, but I knew better.'

'And did you explain any of this to your precious Emily?'

He shook his head. 'I am a coward, and there is your proof of it. I counted her brother as a close friend and comrade, and even he does not know.'

'There is comfort in that, I suppose.' For she doubted she could have survived the shame if David had kept the secret from her as Hendricks had.

'And I have made sure that she will want for nothing, during my life or after it,' he said, as though it would justify his neglect. 'She is my countess, with all the comforts and freedoms that the title allows her. She has free access to the accounts, and she may spend them as she sees fit. All that I have, outside of the entail, is deeded to her, secure in trust.'

'And you think that will be enough to satisfy her, as she waits your return, never knowing what has happened?'

'I doubt she misses me so very much. It has come to my attention that she means to take a lover.'

'And who would tell you such an awful thing?' Since she had only recently learned that he cared at all, it had never occurred to her that her husband might have developed an exaggerated view of her love life.

'Hendricks, my secretary. He is the man who helped you from the tavern two nights ago. He makes frequent trips between us and acts as my eyes and ears at Folbroke Manor. When he comes to town, I question the poor man quite mercilessly about her.' He laughed sadly. 'Recently, it has grown increasingly difficult for him to recount her behaviour. He does not speak of it, of course, but he has a penchant for her as well. And I would not be surprised if she returned his affections.'

'Certainly not!' While Hendricks was not unattractive, the idea that she would choose him over Adrian was so ridiculous that she could hardly stand to hear it.

'Oh, yes, my dear. One does not need eyes to see something like that. When I can get him to speak about her?' Adrian shrugged. 'I can tell that the respect in which he holds her is something more than what one would normally find in a servant. I force him to sit with me, share a brandy to loosen his tongue and tell me of her exploits. And through him, I have come to believe that I have quite the cleverest wife a man could wish for.'

'Except that you think her unfaithful to you.'

Emily could see a muscle tightening in his jaw, as though the matter bothered him more than he was willing to admit. 'I merely have realistic expectations of her. I abandoned her. And I have no intention of ever returning. If I deserved her fidelity, I would be with her this evening. But I will not saddle her with the care of an invalid. Nor do I wish to live at her side as an affectionate brother, leaving her untouched to spare her the risk of bearing my ill-formed whelps.'

'But have you not considered? If you continue in this way, your heir is likely to be sired by another man.'

'Do you think I have not realised the fact?' He bit out the words, sharp and cold. 'If she chooses her lovers with the care that she takes with the rest of my business, the child will be strong and sighted. But if I were to get her with child, there is no telling what might happen. And it would leave her stuck with the care of me. She might as well have two infants for all the use I am likely to be in a few short years.' He laughed mirthlessly. 'Would you like to go and tell her that she must wipe my chin when the spoon cannot find my mouth? Or put me in leading strings so that I can find my own bedchamber?'

'I have watched you, and it is not as bad as all that,' she snapped back. 'You manage quite well on your own, when you are in familiar surroundings.'

'But I have no evidence that she will adjust as well as you have when faced with my disability. You have been unusually understanding, and our arrangement, pleasant though I hope it is for you, is a temporary one. But she should not be put through the bother of a lifetime with me.' He closed the locket and put the picture back into his pocket.

'Nor, apparently, should she be put to the bother of asking her what she wishes.'

'It is what I wish that concerns me,' he said. 'I do not

wish my heir to be blind, nor my wife to look on me with pity, knowing how easy it is to hide the truth from a husband who cannot see her.'

'You do not trust her to be honest.' And, in truth, she was not.

'I would much rather she cuckold me when I am not present than when I am.' He laughed again. 'Either way, I cannot see it.'

'You are horrible.'

'One more proof that my wife is better off without me.'

Adrian was laughing at her, and at their marriage. 'And have you thought, even for a moment, how she might feel to be abandoned, with no explanation? She blamed herself.' She wiped the first stray tear from her eyes with her sleeve, reminding herself that it was unladylike and childish, and that there was no way to know what his wife thought. So she added, 'Or so I would expect.'

He was watching her intently. Or rather he was listening. She could tell by the little cock of his head that he had noticed her stifled sob. 'You are thinking of your own marriage again, aren't you?'

'Perhaps.'

'And I promised that I would give you no reason.' He gathered her close and kissed her upon the forehead, and then the cheek. And then the mouth again, his tongue moving against hers slow and soothing and then faster, as though he meant to tease her back to happiness. He whispered against her lips, 'Let me take the hurt away.'

She could not tell any more who he spoke to. Did he

mean to make her forget? Or did he need to be free of his darling Emily, who, even now, could be lying in the arms of his most trusted friend?

It did not matter. She wanted the same thing he did: for the pain she had carried for so long to go away, and to feel needed and wanted by the one who held her. 'Yes,' she whispered back.

'If you allow me into your bed tonight, I will prove to you that it is possible to meet both my needs and yours. You will have much pleasure and no regrets tomorrow, I promise.'

Emily put her arms around his neck and clung to him, caring for nothing but the feel of his body, close to hers after so long. 'As long as we can be together, that is enough.'

Chapter Ten

'Adrian, please. No more. It is almost dawn and I swear I am exhausted.' Emily laughed, for she had never thought to speak those words, and certainly not to her husband.

'Are you sure, minx?' His hand stole between her legs again, cupping her sex under his palm. 'Although you have left me too weak for another go, I do not think it is possible for a woman to grow too tired for this. Let us see, shall we?'

And it seemed she would know soon enough, for his fingers moved upon her again, as they had so many times since she had led him to her bed.

He had not allowed her to undress him, for he'd claimed that when changing without a valet, he preferred his clothes laid out in a way that ensured he could find them again.

She had watched in eager anticipation as he revealed

without shame the body she had only glimpsed before. The years had not changed him, and she was glad of it. He was as muscular as she remembered, large and strong in ways that made her tremble to the core to look on him.

He had come to her side, kneeling on the edge of her bed and peeled her gown away from her as easily as he had the night before, kissing her face and her body, then toppling her back on to the mattress, his nakedness blending with hers in a tangle of arms and legs and fingers and tongues. He had licked and stroked her to ecstasy more times than she could remember, and spent himself in her hands, between her breasts, and between her thighs, touching her sex with his in a way that was very close to heaven. And then they had slept together, through the night, skin to skin, so close and familiar that they might have been sharing one body.

But not close enough. As he touched her now and dipped inside of her with the tip of his finger, she imagined him entering her, taking her as she had always wanted. She pressed herself against his hand, urging him deeper and remembering the size of him resting heavy in her hands the night before. 'You are bigger than that,' she whispered. And then she gasped, for he had slipped another finger, spreading them inside of her, stretching and moving faster and faster. And she discovered that she was not too tired after all, losing herself all over again in the miraculous maelstrom that she had come to expect from his lovemaking.

'There, my darling,' he said with a smile. 'Admit I was right. Your body wakes at my touch.'

Emily put her arms around his neck and kissed him for what must have been the hundredth time that night. 'And now it would like to sleep at your touch as well. The fire is dying and the sun is rising, but it is still several hours until breakfast. And perhaps the servants would welcome the quiet.' For he had reminded her frequently that he could not see her response, and that it pleased him to hear her cry out.

But now he kissed her gently upon the cheek and disentangled her arms from his neck. 'I had not realised it was so late. You must have your rest.'

She reached out for him, but he had already turned from her, feeling along the edge of the bed and then taking the three steps from the corner that would lead him to the chair with his clothes. 'You are leaving me?' She sat up enough to see the clock upon the mantel. 'It is just past four,' she admitted, with a yawn. 'You can have no other commitments at this hour. Must you go?'

He chuckled. 'If I am honest with myself, probably not. When you know me, you will see that I am the most idle of creatures. I sleep the days away, and my evenings are spent much as you saw the first one.' He pulled on his shirt, tied his cravat in a rough knot, and came back to her, reaching to find her, and kissing her outstretched hand. 'But since I am a wastrel and a rake, it would be better for your reputation if I were not seen leaving this place after breakfast, satisfied by more than a hearty meal.'

She sighed, for perhaps now was the right time to tell him that it did not matter in the slightest. But while they had shared a bed for hours, and done more together than she had ever expected, he had not succumbed enough to do the deed. Nor would he be likely to, if she made him angry.

When she did not answer he said, 'Have you fallen back to sleep?'

'I am merely hoping that if I do not agree, you will not leave.' Because this was how it was supposed to be. How it should have been from the first. The two of them together, sharing the night and greeting the dawn.

'I must go, so that I might return again. And before then, I must have a change of linen and a shave, if you wish me to be the presentable man you want, and not the base ruffian you found me.' He released her hand and returned to the business of dressing. Then he said, casually, as though he did not wish to presume the invitation, 'If you are not busy, of course. And if you desire more of my company. My nights are not empty, but they are not so full that I would not be willing to dedicate them to you.'

He probably meant, if she rejected him, to slip back to the place she had found him, and his inevitable doom. 'No.' She climbed out of the bed to come to his side.

'You refuse me?'

'I refuse to allow you to fill your evenings with anything but me,' she said, twining her arms about him and kissing him again. 'I will meet with you again, as often as you like, night or day, it does not matter to me. I have but one condition.'

He smiled and hugged her. 'I am yours to command.'

'For the duration of our acquaintance, you must not frequent gaming hells or taverns or any other low haunts like the one I found you in. While you may not think yourself worthy of better company, I do not find it flattering to be lumped in with such as that.'

Adrian gave a small laugh, and for a moment she was sure that he would tell her in no uncertain terms that their short acquaintance gave her no right to dictate terms to him. And then he said, 'Well played, madam. In three days, you have succeeded in doing what my friends and family have attempted for years. Of course, they might have had more success in reforming me had they the bait you offer. If you wish me to, I will leave off my vices, for a time, in exchange for the pleasure of your company.'

'And there must be no more talk of seeking an end to your life or dying young by misadventure. You must assure me that whatever happens between us, you will die in bed, at an advanced age.'

'I can hardly be expected to guarantee my own longevity.'

'But you can safeguard what time you have for my sake.' She ran a finger along his chest before buttoning his vest over it. 'I will brook no talk of doom, nor do I wish you threatening to step in front of a dray horse, should I do something that displeases you.' She kissed his chin, nestling her naked body against him and feeling his spirit weaken as his body grew hard.

He groaned and pushed her away, firmly back on her own two feet. 'None of that, then. If I mean to leave you, I will not be able, should you begin again.'

'I will not let you go until you promise. I could not bear it, I swear.'

He leaned against a bedpost, grunting as he pulled on his boots. But he was smiling. 'Very well. To remain secure in your affections, I will do as you ask. Now tell me where to find a bell pull so that I might summon a ride home.'

When she offered to help him, he kissed her firmly on the lips, leading her back to the bed. 'You need not rise. I will find my own way, with some small amount of help. And I dare say your servants must grow used to it. I expect they will see me often from now on.'

Adrian reached his own doorstep without a stumble, handing his coat and stick to a waiting footman. This morning, it was almost a relief to be unable to read the expression on the man's face. If he could see, he was sure that he would find the servant smirking at the master for coming in with the dawn with a smile on his face and smelling of a woman's cologne.

He inhaled deeply. *Lemons, again.* His mouth watered at the thought of her. Or perhaps it was because he had barely eaten. He would have a wash, a shave and a hearty breakfast.

Adrian went to his room and pulled back the curtains, seeing the glow of the rising sun, and felt the first warmth hit his face as his valet came to prepare him for the day.

When Hendricks came to him, several hours later, he swore he could hear the man's shocked intake of breath at finding him upright and taking eggs and kippers at the little table beside the window.

'Come in, Hendricks.' He made a welcoming gesture in the general direction of the door and indicated the chair on the other side of the table. 'Bring the post and *The Times* and help yourself to a cup of tea. And try to contain your astonishment. I swear, I heard your jaw drop as you crossed the threshold.'

'You must admit that it is unusual for me to find you awake, my lord.'

'I am sober as well. And fully dressed. Of course, what I mean to do with all the extra time, I have no idea. I suspect I have put my valet to a great deal of bother, only to spoil my cravat by napping through the afternoon. But what can be done?'

'You are in a better mood today, I see.' His secretary was using his typically mild-mannered voice, but there was a hint of something in it that almost seemed like censure.

'And what if I am?'

'It is rare enough to be worthy of comment. The last time I greeted you cheerfully before noon, you threw a bookend at me.'

'I apologise.' He had been suffering that day from the headache that sometimes accompanied his troubles. Or, if he was more honest with himself, he had been suffering the after-effects of the gin. In either case, it had been no reason to take it out on Hendricks. 'If you felt then as I do today, then I had no right to spoil the mood.' He reached for his tea, and felt Hendricks stay his hand.

'Excuse me, my lord. It has been incorrectly prepared for you. Someone has put lemon in it this morning.'

Adrian grinned. 'And two sugars. Tart, and yet very sweet. Just as I requested it. Never mind the post. I doubt there is anything in it that I care about. But if you could read me the news of the day, I would be most grateful.'

Chapter Eleven

The vigour with which Adrian had started the day had
faded by noon. He might have stood the fatigue if there
had been a way to occupy himself. But with no word
from Emily or his mysterious new lover, there was nothing in the mail that required his attention. And although
the news was interesting, it gave him the familiar feeling
of restlessness to hear it. If he refused his chance to be
involved with the making of laws, he had no real need to
keep abreast of current events. He soon grew frustrated
with the paper and waved his secretary away.

When Hendricks was gone, Adrian roamed his small
rooms like a lost soul. He requested an early lunch, which
he promptly regretted, for the food lay heavy in his stomach. Then he went back to his bedchamber, and lay down
upon the bed, closing his eyes and falling into an uneasy
doze.

He dreamed of *her*, of course. And in those dreams,

he could see her and call her by name. When they had lain together, near exhausted from love-making, he had asked her what she wished to be called, if she would not give him her name.

She had laughed and said, 'Anything you like. Or nothing at all. While I appreciate endearments, I have learned to live without them.'

And it had angered him. For while some women could turn petulant if not given jewels, the woman at his side deserved to be showered with words of love, and yet had been forced to manage with none.

But then she had said, 'But I do seem to enjoy attention that is physical in nature.'

'Do you, now?' He laughed again and moved to touch her, eager to give her what she hinted at. And a name for her had popped easily into his mind. He pushed it away, remembering that though he might imagine what he liked as they made love, he must guard his tongue. She knew too much already about his life and marriage to call her by the name that was always close to his thoughts. It would be an insult to what they shared.

But in his sleep he was loving a woman that was a perfect blend of what he had and what he wanted. Though it should have been the happiest of dreams, and one that he wanted never to end, he could not shake the feeling that the happiness would not last.

And then, at the penultimate moment of his fantasy, there was the sound of something heavy moving in the hall. And of men, grunting under the weight of it, and muffled curses as someone banged an arm or pinched a finger.

Adrian rose and stalked across his room, opening the door with such force that it would have slammed against the wall had it not met with an obstruction. 'What the devil is going on out here? Do you not realise that I am trying to sleep?'

'My lord, if you will excuse us, there is a delivery.' They were trying to manoeuvre something past him, towards the sitting room. 'We were instructed to place it in the corner, by the window.'

'Not by me you weren't,' he said, and heard the footman take an involuntary step back and the burden bumping against the walls in a way that must have scratched the paper from them.

'It is from… She said you would not mind.' There was a tiny stammer at the beginning of the sentence, as though they were unsure how to broach the rest of it.

'She?' There could be only one she that would be so motivated. Whatever it was was probably offered as a 'thank you' for their extremely active night. He should accept it in the spirit it was given, no matter what it might be. 'Well, if she insists that it must go in my sitting room, who am I to argue?' *Other than the owner of the room, of course.*

'Very good, my lord. If you would stand back, just for a moment?' From the sound of his voice, Parker, the footman, was fading under the weight of the thing he carried, but made no move to proceed without his master's permission. The man had made the mistake, when first he'd arrived, of trying to touch Adrian and move him manually out of the way of a delivery. But he had learned with the sharp rap of a cane on his knuckles to keep his distance and allow my lord his space.

Adrian raised his hands and stepped back to give them room to pass.

There was more grunting, and the sound of the two footmen manoeuvring a piece of furniture, followed by the instructions to a third man to 'Get the stool as well'.

When things settled down, Adrian folded his arms and demanded, 'What is it?'

'A pianoforte, my lord.'

'A what?'

'A pianoforte. She said that we might have some difficulty with it, but that it was the smallest one she could find.'

Adrian waved his hands as they began to repeat. 'Never mind. I heard you the first time. But what the hell am I supposed to do with the thing? The woman must be mad—take it away, immediately.'

'There is a message, my lord.' Hendricks spoke from the doorway, for doubtless there was little space left in the room for him.

'Really. Well, then? Speak.'

'She said you would likely object to it. And to inform you, when you did, that you needed something to occupy your days, since idle hands are the Devil's tools.' Hendricks sounded faintly amused, as he could afford to do, being well out of reach of my lord's cane.

Adrian glared into the sitting room, then followed in

the wake of the servants and the unwanted gift. His lady had been happy enough with the Devil's tools when he'd left her. Perhaps she was afraid that he would use them on another, if she did not fill every minute of his life. 'And I suppose, if I send it away…'

'The note says she will find something larger, since simple presents do not seem to entertain you.'

He imagined her voice, framing those words with a hint of disapproval. 'If her man is still waiting, tell him that I will be by this evening to deliver my thanks in person. I would go now, but there is a large piece of furniture blocking my way to the door.'

'Very good, my lord.'

The men cleared away, leaving him alone with his present. And it was as though he could sense the interloper in the room, without even approaching it. He could feel the faint vibrations of the strings inside, for they still hummed with the recent disturbance.

He walked towards it, bumping into the corner and hearing the hollow rap of his cane against its body, running his hand along the side and hoping that she had not wasted money on some gold, heavily ornamented monster of an instrument. It felt simple enough. Rectangular, and with the slightly sticky feel of varnish rather than paint.

So she thought he should keep busy. Clearly, she did not understand what it meant to be a gentleman. His status in society removed the whole point of an occupation. He was not supposed to make work for himself. And many of the things that might have kept him entertained were quite lost to him, now that his eyes were gone. Even gaming had lost its lure. He could no longer read the cards without help, and his need to touch the face of the dice, to feel the spots and assure himself of the roll, was often taken as cheating by his opponents.

He sat down on the bench and laid his hands on the ivory keys, depressing one to hear the tone of it, and depressing his spirit as well. It would need continual tuning, of course. These things always did. But was he expected to know by listening whether it was right or wrong?

He walked his fingers up a scale and sighed, already bored with it in a few short notes. He laboriously picked out a folksong, and then a familiar hymn. The tunes were thin, and he was sure that a talented musician would be searching for seconds and thirds, and chords, finding harmonious combinations by trial and error.

What had he taken from the few music lessons of his youth? Damn little. While his mother had thought it a good idea to give him some understanding of the arts, his father had thought it a waste of time. The clock on the mantel chimed a quarter past the hour. It was just as it had been when he was a boy. He had been sitting at the instrument for only a few moments, and already he was stiff, bored and aching to leave it behind.

'A visitor to see you, my lord.' Abbott had entered with the announcement, and Adrian looked up with eagerness, forgetting for a moment that he had not accepted a guest in months as his condition had deteriorated.

'Mr Eston.'

'Damn and hell.' Emily's brother, and the last man on the planet he wished to see. 'Put him off. Any excuse you like, I do not care.'

'He will not be denied. He says that he means to wait in the entry until he meets with you, either coming or going.'

It sounded very like his old friend David, who in comparison to Adrian had both the patience and morals of a saint. 'Give me a moment, and then show him in.'

When he heard the door close, he hurried across the room to the brandy decanter, filling a glass with such speed that he spilled some on his sleeve. Even better. The smell of the liquor burned in his nostrils, making an attempt at the appearance of drunkenness more obvious. For good measure he dipped his fingers into the glass and sprinkled more of it onto his coat then took a mouthful and swished it about a bit before swallowing. Then he went back to sprawl in a chair by the fireplace with the decanter in one hand and the half-empty glass in the other, barking his shin against the piano bench on the way, then sitting down again just as the door opened.

He looked up as though the hulking shadow in the doorway seemed the least bit familiar, and raised his glass in salute. 'David, it has been so long.'

'Over a year,' his brother-in-law grunted at him.

'And what brings you to London?'

'I have come to fetch you home.'

'Why, my dear sir, I am home.' He waved the glass to encompass the room, spilling more of the contents in the process. 'Please, avail yourself of my hospitality. A drink, perhaps?'

'It is just gone noon, Adrian,' David said with disgust. 'Far too early for brandy.'

'But this is a special occasion, is it not? We have established that you do not visit often. To see you now is a cause for celebration.' To see him at all would be more of a miracle. But for now, his unfocused gaze and unwillingness to meet his friend's eye would be blamed on a guilty nature and the glass in his hand.

Eston grunted again, and he did not need eyes to guess the expression of distaste on the man's face. 'You celebrate too often, as it is.'

'There is much reason to make merry, for London is a fine town.'

'But not so fine that you would bring my sister to it.'

'I did not think she would enjoy it. You said often enough, before we married, that she was a simple girl.'

'She is a woman, now. And she is here in town.' David paused to give significance to the next words. 'But she is not staying with me.'

Adrian gave an uneasy laugh. 'Is that so?'

'She has taken rooms, and refuses to tell me where. I assume that she is using them to receive someone that she does not want me to meet.'

'I do not mind her coming to town. Nor have I forbidden her from socialising. There is money enough to take lodgings of her own, should she choose to. And there is hardly space enough here, should she want to come to me.'

'If there is money enough to maintain two residences,' David said with irritation, 'then there is also money enough to get a town house large enough to share.'

'But would that allow her the privacy she seeks?' Adrian said with mock innocence.

David made a noise of exasperation. 'Why should it matter to you? She is your wife and should not require more privacy than you wish to give her.'

Adrian took a swig of his brandy, and waved his other hand, as if the concept were too much for his addled brain. 'Well then, we are in agreement. I wish to allow her as much privacy as she wants, and to allow myself the same.'

'So it does not bother you that she has taken a lover?'

There would be no way of avoiding the truth if David insisted on sharing it with him. Adrian poured himself another brandy and drank deep, pretending that he cared for nothing but the spirit, ignoring the tightening in his guts. 'And who might that be?'

'I do not know his name,' David said. 'But I ran into her today, shopping on Bond Street. And it was obvious what she has been doing with the days she has been absent from my lodging. She positively glowed.'

'I am encouraged by her continued good health,' Adrian said absently, feeling both relieved and discouraged by the sketchy information.

'It is not health I am referring to, you drunken ninny,' David snapped back, all patience gone. 'I have never seen my sister looking thus. She has been with a man.'

Adrian sipped his drink, looking down into it as

though he could see it. 'And I have been with a woman. I can hardly blame her, David. You know we are estranged.'

'But I do not know the reason for the separation.'

He took another drink from his glass. 'Perhaps not. But it is no business of yours. It is a matter between my wife and myself.'

'And now it is a matter between you and me. You have made no effort to be a husband to her, and now she is likely to shame herself and you with a public affair.'

'With my blessing,' Adrian said, gritting his teeth.

David swore. And then the shifting shadows seemed to indicate him stepping closer, towering over Adrian as he sat by the fire. 'You have been with Emily for three years, and it is clear that you do not mean to get her with child or show her even the slightest modicum of respect. If she looks elsewhere for affection, it is quite possible that your heir will be illegitimate, and then all will know you for a fool, and my sister for a whore.'

Adrian stared into the faint orange glow that marked the ashes from the previous night's fire. 'I think there is little doubt already that I am a fool. And as for her reputation?' He shrugged. 'She is my wife. Any child of hers will be my heir, no matter who his father might be.'

'Are you saying you cannot stir yourself sufficiently to care for Emily that you would be with her long enough to ensure the parentage of your children? If you had so little regard for her, then why did you marry her?'

Adrian drank again. 'Perhaps I never for a moment

wanted her. But I saw no way out of it. My future was sewn up tight by my parents and by yours, before I had any say in it. I am willing to abide by my obligations. But it is a bit much to expect me to do it with a light heart.'

'You selfish bastard,' David said with disgust. 'I remember you of old, Adrian. And I thought you near to fearless. Now, you are telling me that you lacked the nerve to stand up to a slip of a girl and trapped her in a sham of a marriage rather than set her free to find the love she deserved.'

'It is not as though she gained nothing by marrying me,' he muttered. 'She has the land.'

'You have the land,' David reminded him. 'And she has the running of it.'

'And a fine job she does,' he nodded, smiling. 'In reward, I have given her the freedom to find love where she likes. That is what you wished for her, did you not?'

'But it is not what she wishes,' David insisted. 'She adores you, Adrian. At least, she did when you wed her.'

'She gave no sign of it, at the time,' he answered. Not that he had made any great effort to discern the feelings of the woman he had married. But suppose there had been some affection there that he had been too thick to notice? The tiny portrait in his pocket seemed to grow heavier at the thought.

'I know her, even better than I know you. She was too shy to say so, but she was overjoyed at the match. And at the time, she had great hopes that you would learn to love her as well. Emily wanted more than what you have given her.' Now David spoke more gently. 'When I press her about the estrangement, she claims to value her freedom. But I can see the look in her eyes. She wants a husband and children more than your estate. And though she might settle for any man willing to show her affection, her heart is not involved. There is a chance, if you return to her now, that it is not too late. Her *tendre* for you could be rekindled.'

Dear God, no. 'And what would make you think that I had any desire for such?' It was the last thing he needed to hear, now of all times. Sometimes it seemed that his only source of consolation was that his death would be a relief to her. But suppose it was otherwise?

'Perhaps I think you should care less about what you desire, and stop behaving like some stupid young buck, fresh from the classroom and eager to indulge every whim. Go back to your wife before she sinks as low as you have and cares for naught but meeting her own needs.'

'Now see here,' Adrian snapped back, feeling the beginnings of a cloud over his thoughts from the brandy he had bolted. 'What I do or do not do with your sister is no affair of yours. The only reason it bothers you, I think, is because you had some designs on my land yourself. See it as an extension of your own park, do you? Hunting and fishing and riding on my property as though you own it. You must think that I will go the way of my short-lived ancestors, and that when I am gone, you will twist my heir around your little finger.' He laughed and took another gulp, letting his imagination run wild. 'That'll be much harder to do if the whole thing passes to some cousin, won't it? If there is no heir, your sister will be put off to dower, and your plans will all be for naught.' It was a disgusting picture. And he wondered if there was any truth in it.

David cursed and knocked the glass from his hand onto the hearth. 'It is only affection for Emily that keeps me from calling you out.'

'And I might say the same. If any other man had dared to come into my study to tell me how to organise my life and my marriage, I'd have run him through.'

He could almost hear David's eyes narrow. 'You needn't fear that in the future, Adrian. All who once claimed you as a friend are gone, driven off by your shameful behaviour. But if they still existed, they would also tell you that you are a sot and a wastrel and they are embarrassed to know you. You lose yourself in liquor and whores, intent on destroying yourself like your father and grandfather did before you, little heeding the pain you heap on your wife and friends. I rue the day that a union of our families was suggested. I do not need access to your land, and will keep within the boundaries of my own estate, if the thought of my trespassing bothers you so. From now on, I will live as a stranger to you.'

'At last! He means to leave me alone!' Adrian hoped that volume would make up for the lack of true feeling in the dismissal.

'And it is a shame, Adrian, for I once thought of you almost as a brother. I welcomed the connection between us and hoped that a wedding would bring you happiness, moderate your character and be a benefit to Emily. I have proved myself a bigger fool than you are for putting my trust in you.'

His childhood friend spoke with such disappointment that he almost admitted the truth. But what good would that do? The man would be just as angry that poor Emily had been tricked into such an ill-fated match. 'You must have known,' Adrian said softly, 'that there was a chance that you were wrong. That blood might tell, and I would be no better than the rest of my family.'

'But I knew you. Or thought I did. And I was sure, at one time, that you had a heart to be touched. I am beginning to suspect that it is not the case.'

Adrian hid his confusion in a cold laugh that he knew would enrage his guest. 'Then you are learning me right, after all these years,' he said looking up at the hazy spectre of his oldest friend, looming over him.

'Very well, then. The interview is at an end, as is the last of our friendship. You have treated my sister abominably. You have scorned my efforts to intervene. What is likely to occur from all this will be entirely on your head.'

And even without sight, Adrian could chart David's passage out of the rooms by the slamming of the doors.

Chapter Twelve

'Hendricks!' Adrian bellowed. If the man was still in, there would be no way for him to escape the sound of his master's voice.

'My lord?' His response was so prompt that Adrian wondered if the secretary had been listening at the door.

'I was just forced to undergo an excruciating fifteen minutes with Eston. Am I mistaken, Hendricks, or do I pay you to prevent such things?'

'I am sorry, my lord.'

If he wished to be rational, he would admit that it had been the distraction of the piano delivery that had left the doors open and allowed the guest to enter, not any carelessness on Hendricks's part. But the excess of spirits was making him irritable, as was the disapproving sniff that Hendricks gave at the spilled brandy. Adrian set the decanter aside. 'To avert questions about my behaviour, I let him think me drunk. I have most likely ruined this coat by dousing myself with liquor. But he felt the need to tell me that my wife has taken a lover. What do you know of the situation?'

'Nothing, my lord.' But the man said 'nothing' with such a lack of conviction that he might as well have said everything.

'Really. But you have seen her recently, I trust?'

'Yes, my lord. This morning.'

'And how did she look, when you last spoke with her?'

'Well.'

'Is that all, Hendricks? For her brother implied that she was looking, perhaps, too well.'

Adrian's comment should have been incomprehensible. But Hendricks seemed to understand it perfectly. 'I did not notice anything unusual about her, my lord.' It was a pitiful attempt to hide the truth.

'And where was she, when last you saw her?'

Hendricks paused, as though he could not seem to remember his story, and said, 'At her brother's town house, my lord.'

'How strange. For she has not been in residence there for several days.'

Hendricks sighed. 'At her rooms, my lord.'

'So you have seen them, then?' He resisted the desire to add the word *Aha*. 'I suppose you have been there several times.'

'Yes, my lord.' He sounded glum now, as though any good spirits that the lady might have gained through his visits were not shared.

As an afterthought, Adrian asked, 'As I remember it, Hendricks, you wear spectacles, do you not?'

'Yes, my lord,' said Hendricks, clearly baffled as to what this had to do with anything.

And there went his hopes that the next Earl of Folbroke would be unencumbered by difficulties with vision. Still, some sight was better than none. 'Her brother David seemed most concerned at the damage to her reputation, should it be known that she is setting up housekeeping with a man. If she wished some space of her own, it is a shame that she has not seen fit to ask her husband for permission.'

'Did you expect her to? It has been long since you have spoken to her—she no doubt assumed that you would not care.' Hendricks had answered a trifle too quickly with this, and altered his tone to be less censorious before adding, 'If you wish to see her today, I could arrange it for you.'

'It merely surprises me that she has not sought me out. If she cannot visit her own husband when she is scant miles from him, then it gives credence to her brother's theory.'

'She did visit you, my lord, on the day she arrived in town. As you remember, I came to fetch you.'

And pulled me from another woman's arms and dragged me home, insensible. Touché, *Hendricks,* touché. 'Since she did not return, I did not think the matter was important.'

'Perhaps it is because she has been spurned and avoided for such a long time that she has no more desire to try.' His secretary's voice was sharp and scolding. And there could be no questioning his meaning. 'At this point in time, perhaps it is up to you to seek her.'

'Do you presume to tell me how to handle my marriage?'

'Of course not, my lord.' But the tone said just the opposite.

'You might as well do it, for it seems quite a popular activity this week.' He gave a vague gesture towards the writing desk. 'Draft a letter to Emily. I will see her this evening at six. Do it quick, man, before I sober sufficiently from Eston's visit to realise what a mistake I am making.'

'See her, my lord? Do you wish me to explain the unlikelihood of that? For I believe your condition still a mystery to her.'

For a moment he *had* forgotten. Damn that strange woman for getting under his skin and making him think, even for an instant, that his life could be ordinary.

'No. Emily has no clue. Unless you have told her.'

'You forbade me.' It was a comfort to hear the resignation, and the resolution, in that sentence and the lack of even a fraction of a second's hesitation. Whatever else he might be doing, it was plain that Hendricks followed some of his instructions to the letter, no matter how unwise he thought them.

Adrian shook his head. 'After all this time, there are no simple words to describe to her what has happened, or to explain why I hid the truth. It will be easier when we are face to face to explain things, so that there can be no mistaking. It is not as if my lack will come as a severe shock to her. I am not disfigured in any way, am I?' He touched his own face, suddenly unsure. Perhaps time had made him an ogre, and the servants were too kind to remark on it.

'No, sir.'

'Then I will explain to her, once she arrives. It is time, I think, that there be some truth between us.'

'Very good, my lord.'

'Mr Eston, my lady.'

When the footman announced her brother, Emily was enjoying what she'd thought was a well-earned cup of tea. With her morning's shopping and calls, she had taken what she'd hoped were the first steps to sorting out her husband's problems. Or perhaps they were steps towards encouraging him to do so, for she doubted there would be any change in his character without full co-operation from the man himself.

But since no one knew of her location, she had not expected visitors other than Hendricks. And she certainly had not expected to see her brother. 'David?' Thinking of the confrontation she expected from him, his name came out of her mouth in a breathless whimper that made her sound guiltier than she was over her behaviour. 'What are you doing here?' There, she noted with some relief. The strength returned to her when she turned the challenge back to him.

'I have come to see what you are doing here, and who you are doing it with.' Her brother signalled the footman for another cup and sat in the chair opposite her. His presence was so commanding that she thought for a moment that he had invited her to the room to explain herself.

'It is not necessary for you to watch over me. Nor is it your place,' she reminded him. 'I am both grown and married.'

'If you can call what you share with Adrian a marriage,' he responded.

'Says the man who is the same age as my husband, but has no wife of his own.'

The mention of this seemed to make him uncomfortable, so he turned the argument hurriedly back to her. 'It is your husband I wish to speak of, and not my nonexistent wife. I have been to see Adrian, since you have not.'

'That was not necessary.'

'I feel it was,' he said, looking around him at her rooms. 'I saw you this morning, shopping in Bond Street.'

'I remember,' she said coolly. 'I greeted you, did I not?'

'But you were behaving strangely. Secretively. There is but one reason that I can think of to explain such behaviour.'

'Oh, I seriously doubt that,' she said. Emily could feel herself begin to blush, which would make her look even more guilty. But there was little to be done to stifle the sudden and rather graphic memories of what she had been up to in the days since she had moved from her brother's house.

'You have taken up with some man.' He was staring at her clothing, which was too casual to accept any but a lover, and the flush of her skin. And God forbid that he should look in the bedroom, for he might see the sheets, still rumpled from last night's activities.

She took another sip of tea to hide her confusion. 'Hardly, David.'

'And you have rented rooms so that the meetings could be done in secret.'

'Not much of a secret, clearly, since you have followed me to them. Was that how you found me?' But he had clearly not looked too closely into the matter, if he had not identified the man in question.

He showed no sign of noticing her censor. 'I questioned my coachman, since you seem intent on using my vehicle as your own. And he admitted taking your baggage to this place. But we are not discussing my behaviour. It is yours that is in question. I waited outside this morning. And in the dim light, I saw someone creeping away from here. He was in the carriage and away before I could get a look at him.'

'Oh, David,' she said, wincing with embarrassment at this further complication of her plans. 'Why now? You have not given a thought to my behaviour in years. It is not as if I did not have admirers before.'

'But you were not serious about them. And even if you were, that was in the country. It was not as if anyone was likely to notice you there.'

So she had been out of sight and out of mind to him as well, had she? 'I suspect it was easier for you, when

I remained there. But you could not expect me to avoid London for ever, could you?'

'Perhaps not. But I expected that when you returned to town, you would be circumspect in your behaviour. If you cannot manage your reputation, you will come home immediately.'

'I will not.' She thought for a moment. 'And just where do you mean to take me, if I must come home? Not to your house, certainly. I have not lived under that roof since I married.'

'But perhaps you should, if you mean to disgrace the family.'

'I am no longer a member of your family. But if Adrian has a problem, after all this time, then he should be the one to come here, and drag me back to the country.'

'We both know that he will not,' her brother replied with disgust. 'If he exercised the discipline necessary in his own house, then the job would not fall to me. And if you did not go to such lengths to make absence easy for him, he might be forced to return home and see to his business.'

'Then why do you not go to the source of the problem and talk to him? Why do you think it necessary to harass me over the state my marriage?'

'I have been to him,' her brother ground out through gritted teeth. 'I took what I learned to Folbroke, just now. He was already drunk, though it was barely noon. And he showed no interest in my company, nor your presence in town.'

Drinking again? She frowned. Adrian had seemed sober enough when they had been together the previous evening. She had hoped that problem, at least, was in abatement. 'And that was your only fault with him?' For there was a significant matter that her brother had not mentioned.

'Other than his damned stubbornness and bad temper. He barely looked at me the whole time I was there. As though, if he ignored me, he would not have to answer to me.'

'I see.' Her poor brother would be even angrier than she had been when he learned of the trick. 'I expect he liked your interference no better than I do.'

'Is it truly interference to wish that my oldest friend and my dear sister would find happiness with each other, instead of behaving in ways that are a scandal?'

Emily thought of the things that had occurred in these rooms, which, while exciting, were probably some of the least scandalous things her husband had done since their marriage. 'Perhaps we shall. Perhaps I have my own plans to rectify the breach. You must trust that I can manage this. You are not married, and cannot understand what goes on between a husband and wife, even when they are not happy.' She thought for a moment, and smiled. 'Especially when they are not happy. Although it might not seem so, I find that I am quite capable of managing Adrian, now that I have set my mind to try.'

Her brother shook his head. 'You had best manage this quickly, then, for my patience with his behaviour is nearing an end. If you cannot bring him home with you, by God, I will drag him back home by the ear. I cannot stand by any longer and watch him destroy himself, Emily. I simply cannot.'

She could see, by the look in her brother's eyes, that his interference came not from a desire to control, but sincere pain at the way his friend was likely to end. She gave him a pat on the hand. 'Trust me. A little longer. It will be all right. You will see.'

There was the sound of yet another guest, and Hendricks walked into the room, unannounced, as though he were perfectly at home there.

And Emily saw the narrowing of David's eyes, as he came to a conclusion that was not evident to her. 'Mr Hendricks?'

'Mr Eston.' There was a similar narrowing of Hendricks's eyes behind his glasses, as though he answered some unspoken challenge. Then he looked to her. 'My lady, I bring a letter from your husband.'

'Do you, now?' David said, as though he assumed there was some ruse in play.

'I believe he wrote it at your suggestion, sir,' Hendricks said innocently.

'And you were able to deliver it here so quickly without stopping first to find Emily at my town house.'

'Oh, really, David,' she said. 'Mr Hendricks knows the location because he helped me to let it. And if there is a letter from Adrian, you must assume that we are more *simpatico* than you know. Now, if you will excuse me, I wish to read the thing in private.'

'Very well, then.' He shot Hendricks another suspicious look. 'But if I do not hear of a meeting between the two of you within a week, I will go back to Adrian, and tell him what I have seen here. I suspect he will find it of interest.'

When he had left, Emily looked down at the paper in her hand, thoroughly annoyed with her brother for spoiling what she hoped might be a pleasant read. And then she noticed that it was addressed to Emily, and written in the hand of his secretary. She glared back at Hendricks. 'So my lord finally summons me, does he?'

'Yes, Lady Folbroke. And he asked after you. He seemed most interested in your status, and rather ashamed of the length of time since he has last seen you and the fact that he has hidden his blindness.'

She sniffed. 'The pangs of a guilty conscience, more like.'

'He had just received a visit from your brother, and was concerned about the reason you removed from the Eston town house. Mr Eston thinks a gentleman is involved.'

'Too rightly. And with your sudden arrival here, he has concluded that the gentleman is you. What nonsense.'

There was a long pause as Hendricks tried to decide how to respond to his change in status from servant to Lothario. 'Of course, my lady.'

'And my husband's response to this rumour?'

Hendricks held out the letter to her again.

'I see that. And that it is written in your hand. What, in your opinion, was his reaction to rumours of my infidelity?'

'In my opinion?' repeated Hendricks, as though he wished to make it clear that he did not speak for her husband. 'He is jealous, my lady.'

She felt a brief moment of triumph, followed by annoyance. 'So what is sauce for the gander is not sauce for the goose.' She tapped the letter with her nail. 'And has he set an agenda for this meeting?'

'He means to tell you of his problems.'

'And I already know of them. What is meant to come after this grand revelation?'

'I think he means to come to some understanding between you.'

She tossed the paper on to the fire. 'In which I am more discreet and he does not change at all. If that is the case, then I hardly need to stir myself, for I am having no part of that.' She smiled at Hendricks, trying not to look as smug as she felt. 'I am enjoying myself far too much to stop now. And if the thought of my happiness without him causes him discomfort, then all the better.'

'Do you wish to send him a message to that effect?'

'No.' For some reason, Adrian's sudden need to see her had angered her to the point where she could hardly speak, probably because she had worked hard and long to quash any hope that it would ever happen. 'There is no message. If he asks, tell him I have refused. Since he has waited years to summon me, he should not be surprised to find me otherwise engaged on the night he is ready to unburden his soul.'

'Very good.' Hendricks frowned at her as though he did not mean it.

And he was right. It was not good. Her behaviour was foolish and childish. It should have been welcome news to find that he worried about her, pined after her and had worn the paint from her picture through constant handling of it. Instead, it reminded her of all the time that had been wasted. She resented being the afterthought to her husband's infidelities, almost as much as she enjoyed receiving the attention from them. She sighed. 'I am sorry, Hendricks, that I cannot make this easier upon him. His wife is quite out of patience with him. But I will wait upon him here, tonight, as I have done before. Perhaps he will be more free with his thoughts to his lover.'

Chapter Thirteen

Adrian arrived at her rooms that evening, so full of anger and indignation that he did not need to speak to show his mood. It was there in the set of his back, the tightness of his gait, and the staccato rapping of his cane against the parquetry floor. After a moment's hesitation, she went up on tiptoes to kiss him, and he responded with a perfunctory peck upon the cheek.

Then he brushed off her advance as though he could not be bothered with it, tucking his cane under his arm so that he could tug the gloves off his hands, then tossed them into his hat with unusual force.

Emily stepped away. 'I thought, after this morning, that I would receive a better greeting than this. What is the matter?'

'It has been a trying day,' he said with a glare, tapping about the hall to feel the bench beside him and landing the hat on it with a flick of his wrist. 'When I am home,

I prefer peace and quiet, uninterrupted by changes or surprises. But today it was impossible. Someone had taken it upon themselves to give me a pianoforte.'

'Do you like it?' she asked, although she could see by his expression what the answer was likely to be.

'Have I given you any reason to think that I would?'

'You had said that you were idle most days. And I thought, if you had something to occupy the daytime hours, then at night you would not need to go out.'

He closed his eyes and gave the frustrated sigh of a man pushed beyond the edge of his temper. 'Did I not promise you last night that I would not carouse?'

'While we were together, yes. But I am concerned that, once we are parted, you will forget your promise.'

'Once we are parted?' He raised an eyebrow. 'Have you grown tired of my company so soon?'

'It is not that at all,' she said.

'Or perhaps, after only a day or two, you think you have some claim on me, that you would reorder my life to suit you?'

'A single gift is hardly an attempt to reorder your life,' she said.

'And a large gift it is. A large gift placed in a small space. When you know me better, you will find that I do not like the furniture rearranged once I have taught myself the lay of it. And your pianoforte presents more of an obstacle than an opportunity.'

'That is because you have not tried it, I am sure,' she said. 'You do not need your eyes to play it. Once you learn the scales, you will find that you can make music with your eyes open or closed.'

'So it is a gift of charity to the poor blind man, is it?'

'Only if you choose to see it so,' she coaxed. 'Some people quite enjoy playing an instrument.'

'I had quite enough of it, as a boy.'

'You took lessons, then?' For she did not remember hearing of them.

'One or two. And then, in one of my father's rare shows of sense, he fired the music master and freed me from the duty of it. He bought me a fine jumper, instead.' He smiled as though he were remembering. 'And a beautiful beast it was. He could take a fence as easy as walking, and went over the stone walls at the bottom of the yard as though we were flying.'

'But you cannot do such as that any longer,' she said.

'Thank you for reminding me,' he answered. 'Neither can I shoot, for it would be a torture to the animals I hunted, more than a sport. From my father and grandfather I learned the dangers of pretending to be a gentleman—I no longer bother to try. And without your help, I have lasted longer as a rogue than either of them.'

She put her hand on his arm. 'You might think I am showing a lack of faith in your abilities, but we both know that it is a matter of luck and not skill that has brought you some of the way. It is not that I have a claim on you, so much as I would not wish the fate you seek on anyone.'

'And I have no desire to be led about on a pony, as though I am an infant. Nor do I wish to spend the rest of my life in the parlour, playing scales. Next you will be encouraging me to weave baskets or make buttons. Or maybe I can learn needlework, like an old lady. I swear, you are as bad as those meddling souls that incarcerate the sightless and train them like dogs.'

'Hardly,' she said. 'And I have been to the blind school here, if that is what you mean. It is not so bad.'

His eyes narrowed. 'It is not a school, my dear. Call it by its right name. The Blind Asylum at Southwark.'

'It is called an asylum only because it is meant as a place of safety.'

'Is that what you think? For I went there as well, while I could still see the place. And to me, it seemed as though it was meant to keep the sighted safe from the presence of those of us who are less fortunate.'

'The children there are clean and well cared for.'

'And taught to do simple trades as befits their intelligence, and their station in life.' He sneered at her. 'They are not taught to read and write and study. They are made useful, and the training is done by men almost as common as they are themselves. My father would have ended his life before getting me, if he had thought that this was the only future that waited.'

'And I am sure he is much more proud to think you gambled and drank and whored your life away, rather than finding some valuable way to occupy your time.' His stubbornness infuriated her. But it was not without cause. Adrian had been a vigorous youth. And one by one, the things that gave him pleasure were becoming impossible. 'If you do not like the pianoforte, then you need not play it,' she said, in a soothing voice. 'I will send someone to remove it tomorrow and that will be the end of it.'

But she could tell by his expression that he was not mollified. She put her arms around his neck and added, 'If that is all that is bothering you.'

'It is not,' he snapped. And then muttered, 'But the rest is no concern of yours.'

'I see.' She gave an audible sigh to let him know that she was pouting, surprised at her desire to try feminine wiles that she was sure must be long withered from disuse.

'It was just that the damned instrument was followed by a visit from my brother-in-law, come to trouble me about my wife's misbehaviour.'

'And of course it annoyed you,' she said with sympathy, stroking his arm. 'It was rather pointless of him to bother you, since you do not care how your wife behaves.'

His head snapped up, as though he had been struck. 'Do not dare to presume what I feel about the woman I married.'

'I presume nothing,' she said with a little laugh of surprise. 'You told me how you felt not twenty-four hours ago. That it did not bother you what she did, and that you had no claim on her fidelity.'

'But that was before she took up publicly with another,' he answered. 'And to think that I trusted the man. It upsets me that he can lie to my face. And it upsets me even more that he does not do a better job of it. I might not be able to see my hand before my eyes, but I can see through him like a piece of tissue.'

'And who might he be?' she asked, for it was clear that Adrian had formed an opinion.

'Hendricks, of course.'

The idea was so ludicrous that she laughed out loud. 'Are you still going on about him? I have met the man, and it hardly seems likely.'

'Oh, I am almost sure of it. He has admitted knowing of her lodgings, and visiting her there. And he is quite clearly uncomfortable around me, as though he is afraid of being caught in some secret.'

'And have you asked your wife what she has to say on the matter?'

'I would have asked, had I been able to persuade her to visit me. I requested her presence this evening and she ignored me.'

'So that is it,' she said. 'You are angry with her and everyone around you must take the blame for it. But you take no part of the fault for yourself, of course.'

'I?' He disentangled her arms from his neck.

'If you had spoken honestly to her before now, she might not have chosen another. And you would be telling her of your displeasure, not some woman that you barely know.'

'That is not true at all,' he argued. 'In my experience, I am doing nothing so unusual. Few men speak to their wives. When they wish to discuss things of importance to them, they seek the company of other men.'

'And when they wish to unburden their souls?' she pressed.

'Then they go to their mistresses. When a woman is paid to do as she is told, she is less likely to disagree. A wife, though she might swear at the altar to be obedient, seldom is. Emily has proven thus. And I would have thought her the most tractable female on the planet. Until today.' He stared up at the ceiling with a furrow in his brow, as though, for all his fine talk, he had never really believed her capable of leaving him.

'And suppose you find yourself with a woman who owes you no obedience at all?' She reached up to touch his face, putting a hand to his forehead and smoothing the lines with her fingers.

'Then I would have a mind to show her a new use for her pianoforte.' He kissed her palm.

'Do you mean to invite her to your home, so that you might play a duet?' she teased.

'More likely I would be inclined to bend her over the stool for her impudence, and love her until she was more agreeable.' His voice was husky, and he pulled her close, kissing her hard until his anger began to dissipate.

She opened her mouth, and let him convince her, marvelling at how little effort it took him to arouse her. A word or two, a kiss, a touch. And she wanted to be his. She pulled away, slow, almost drowsy, and murmured back at him. 'You presume too much, my lord. Do you think you can force all women to submit to your every wish?'

'Not all women,' he whispered back. 'Just you.

Because you do not want chaste duets in the drawing room any more than I want to play a pianoforte. We are physical creatures, you and I. Not made to sit tamely to the side while the rest of the world dances.'

Emily had never thought of herself in that way before. But it was true. She was happier walking his land, visiting cottages and farms, meeting the stock and the people than she would have been sitting with her needlework in the drawing room, waiting for her husband to favour her with a visit. And when he talked to her, rough and low as he was doing now, she felt like a sybarite. The things he suggested made her flush with eagerness and not embarrassment. Instead, she focused her mind on more innocent pursuits. 'If there is music, you would rather dance than play, my lord?'

He considered. 'I have never tried. There has been scant little music in my life, these last few years.' He swept her into his arms as though he heard a waltz and spun her once, bumping her into a chair.

She felt him hesitate, gripped his hand tighter and said, 'A moment, please.' Then she released him, righted the furniture and pulled him into the doorway of the salon. 'Now try again.'

He began more slowly this time, and they took a few steps without incident. 'I will lead,' he said, 'but you must guide me.' He turned her again.

They were nearing a table now. 'Left. No. Right.' The turning had confused her for a moment, and they moved past it, rocking the china ornaments upon it, but not breaking them. 'Now straight back for a bit. And turn again, another right. And there is a circuit of the room.'

He gave her a final flourish and her silk skirts sighed about her legs, and then settled.

Adrian nodded, as though satisfied with their success, and then dismissed it as unimportant. 'Of course, there is no orchestra to keep the beat. And we did not have to navigate a room full of people.'

'Dancers with all their sight cannot manage as well as you have done. It seems I cannot escape a rout without crushed toes and bumped elbows. And I am sure you would find a dance, with lines and patterns, to be easier. A drunken idiot can manage the Sir Roger de Coverley.'

'Thank you for your confidence in me,' he murmured sarcastically. 'But dancing in a crowded room would not be quite so pleasant as holding my partner close like this when we are alone.' He had her now, in his arms, swaying as though he still heard a tune. But they were far too close to be waltzing, their bodies rubbing together until she could feel them both becoming aroused.

'I do not think what we are doing now can be called dancing,' she said a little breathlessly, brushing her breasts against the front of his coat and feeling the roughness of the net bodice against her nipples.

'What would you call it, then?' he asked. His hands bunched in her skirt, pressing their hips together, but his lips brushed lightly against hers.

'I think you are trying to seduce me again.'

One of his hands found the pocket slit in the side of

her skirt, and reached inside to press his palm against the bare skin of her leg. 'Am I likely to be successful?'

She rubbed her cheek against his. 'I think you might be.' She swayed against him, letting him urge her closer, slipping one of her legs between his and drawing her foot up the inside of his calf. He caught her leg between his, tightening his muscles, and she felt the now-familiar rush of feeling, knowing he was close to her, knowing what would come next between them.

She rubbed herself against him with a little moan, and he pushed her back against the edge of a desk, getting some distance between their bodies to put a hand down the loose bodice of her gown. 'You are a most welcoming woman, my dear. Bare under your dress again tonight. I think, if I had a mind to, you would let me take you here.'

'Yes,' she said with a groan, thinking how wonderful it would be if he would lose control.

'I could just hoist up your skirt...'

'Yes...' He was kissing her, short sharp bites on her lips, down her throat.

'Undo a few buttons...'

'Yes...' One hand, tight upon her breast, the other in her skirt, squeezing her leg.

'And I could be inside of you, before anyone was the wiser.' He was holding her body a tantalising inch from his. And she pressed herself down onto his thigh.

'Show me,' she whispered back and pushed her hands between the buttons of his vest, searching to touch skin and not clothing.

'Wait.' He laughed. 'Wait. There is time. We do not need to rush. Let me take you into the bedroom.'

But if they took their time, he would be careful. And while it would be wonderful, it would not be what she truly wanted. 'No. Here, now. Quickly.' She kissed him, deep and wet, pushing her tongue into his mouth, sucking his back into hers.

And for a moment, he stopped resisting her and pulled her hips forwards, wrapping a hand around them to lock her sex to his, grinding against her through their clothing. She wrapped her arms around his neck, lifting herself onto her toes, making it easier to join with him.

Then he pulled his lips from hers and gave a shaky sigh. 'No, my sweet. Let us go lie down and treat each other properly.'

'And suppose I do not wish you to be proper?' she said. 'Suppose I wish you to be rough with me, and finish with me quickly and carelessly, in a public room, because you cannot stand to wait?' She ran her leg up between his thighs until she could feel his manhood and pressed hard against it, rubbing her knee against him until he groaned.

Then he unwrapped her arms from his body, trying to part them. 'You do not understand,' he said. 'It is not that you do not tempt me.'

'Then give me what I want,' she demanded and lifted her own skirt to bare herself, pressing her naked sex against the front of his trousers, so close to him that she wanted to weep with frustration.

Without thinking, he swore and his mouth covered

hers again, and his hand fumbled to open his trousers, pushing the cloth away until they were skin to skin. He parted from her, just enough to mutter, 'Lean back, just a bit.' And now he was resting between her legs, rubbing himself gently against her and peppering her lips with desperate little kisses. 'Just for a moment. Just a taste of you. I will be careful. I promise.'

She smiled, trembling, waiting for the delicious shock of sensation that would soon come. 'You do not have to be careful with me. Never with me. I am yours, Adrian. I love you.'

And then it was over. He jerked away from her so fast that it was as though she had burned him, hurrying to do up his buttons although he was still obviously in need of her. 'I think, my dear, that we had best take supper. Suddenly, I find myself in need of a cooling drink.'

Emily held out a hand to him, remembering too late that he could not see it. But neither could he see her crimson cheeks, or the beginnings of tears. Then she smoothed her skirt back into place and wrapped her arms around herself as a shield against his rejection. 'Do you really? Do you think I will forget my feelings for you? Or do you wish to distract yourself?'

'Both, perhaps.' He looked older than he had a few minutes ago. His face was serious and lined with stress, and his posture stiff and unnatural, as though he was guarding himself from her as well. 'I do not think you understand what you are saying to me, and I do not mean to take advantage of a generosity that is based on lies and suppositions, no matter how pleasant they might be. You do not love me. You cannot.'

'I do,' she cried. 'Do not think to tell me the contents of my heart, just because you wish it to be other than it is.'

'We have known each other for only a few days. And what there has been between us is not love. It is something else entirely.'

'Perhaps that is how it is for you,' she said, 'but I have known you for ever. And for as long as that, I have loved you.'

He had nothing to say to that, and stood a little bit apart from her with a strange, lost look on his face, as though he feared that any direction he might move would be misinterpreted by her, as his other actions had been.

She wanted to gather him close, to kiss his sightless eyes, and to tell him he had no reason to deny her or her love. There was nothing more natural in the world than for him to give in to the temptation and join with her. Her heart ached for it—just as her body ached for the child that he refused to give her.

She took deep, slow breaths, willing the passion in her to subside, leaving cold emptiness in its wake. For a few moments, it had been as if the barriers he kept between them had fallen. He had returned to her, was with her, body and soul. And for that time, no matter what he might claim now, he had been ready not just to make love, but to love her without fear of the future.

But now he was gone again. Hiding from his wife. Hiding from his lover. And even though they shared the same room, she felt lonelier than she had a week ago, when he had seemed as distant from her as a ship on the horizon.

Though it did not matter how she looked, she put on a false smile and said, 'You are right. There is a supper laid for us in the dining room. Let me take your arm, that you might lead me to it.' She put her hand in the crook of his elbow and gave him the direction he needed so that he might walk her to the table. They seated themselves and ate in near silence, with only the occasional nervous comment from him about the tenderness of the vegetables, and his gratitude to the cook for doing such a thorough job of boning the salmon.

When it looked as though he was ready to give a lengthy oration on the dessert, Emily cut him off. 'I am sorry if I upset you.'

'You did nothing of the kind,' he assured her, a little too quickly.

'Of course I did. And I would understand if you did not want to stay with me tonight.'

'Of course I wish to stay,' he said, reaching across the table to grasp her hand, 'but I do not know if it is wise.' And then he squeezed her fingers. 'But I do not know if I want to be wise, if it means losing my time with you.'

'That is a comfort. I promise not to say it again. You needn't worry.' *It.* As though she felt some objectionable thing that needed to be hidden.

'Actually, I would prefer that you are honest with me. It is most refreshing to find a woman who speaks frankly.'

'Thank you,' she said, hating herself for the lies, wanting to scream the truth in his face. *I am your wife. Your Emily.*

Love me.

'It is just that I do not want you to raise your hopes about what can be between us in the end. It is not that I do not…have feelings for you. Strong feelings,' he amended. There was a wistful quality in his voice, as though he were staring through a shop window at something he could not have. 'You are a friend and confidante. Someone I trust implicitly and who trusts me in return. If that is the true definition of a lover, then that is what you are to me. And that is what I wish to be for you.'

Emily stared down into her plate, thinking of how it had been in Derbyshire. Then, such pretty words would have sent her heart racing. He felt strongly for her. He wanted her. She was something like a lover to him. Why could she not be satisfied? Why was that not enough?

Without releasing her hand, he stood, drawing her up with him. From memory, he led the way from the table to the bedroom. He took the time to arrange his clothes as he removed them, but took no such care with hers, opening the buttons at the back of her gown and letting it fall to the floor at her feet. He lifted her out of it and set her upon the bed with a kiss on the lips before sliding his body down hers, taking her breasts with long slow licks, smoothing his hands over her ribs and settling himself between her legs to kiss there, tenderly, worshipfully.

She closed her eyes and gave herself over to his ministrations, the tug of teeth, the gentle probing of fingers, the tentative invasions of his tongue. And she told herself that it was greedy of her to want more when he was giving her something that felt so good. And she knew, from the previous times he'd done it, that what he was doing had the strength to rend her soul from her body and send it crashing back to earth again.

The final pleasure was slow in coming. And when it came, she wept.

Chapter Fourteen

The sun was well up by the time Adrian awakened. He did nothing to acknowledge it for his lover was still sleeping on his arm. The night had been as glorious as the night before, and parts of the night before that. As exciting as the fight in the tavern. And probably almost as dangerous.

I love you.

When she had said it, along with the abject terror it had raised in him had been the ghostly echo of a response in his own heart—how could something as perfect as the time they spent together not have some deeper feeling in it? He smoothed a hand over her curls and she nuzzled him in her sleep.

If she had said nothing, he'd have ignored his intentions and taken her up against the wall in the salon, trusting that she would tell him if they were not alone—he could not have heard a servant's footstep had he tried, his heart had been beating so loudly. Apparently, there was madness in what he felt for her as well.

And then she had said the words, and he'd stopped himself, too near the brink. He'd taken her to dinner, then he'd taken her to bed. And he'd loved her in all the ways he could until he was sure that she had forgotten.

But her pillow was wet with tears. And in her sleep, she had whimpered like a lost child.

She stirred; he ran a soothing hand over her back, wishing that she would sleep again. It felt good to be here and he did not want to go. She rolled off his arm to free it, and he could feel her and see the shadow as she propped herself up on her elbows in the pillows. 'You are not going to run away from me in the dawn?'

'I am afraid it is too late for that already. But I must go soon.'

'Then stay a while longer,' she said. 'Give me time to wash and dress. I will go with you and see you home.'

He frowned. 'There is no need to help me. I am quite capable of managing a carriage ride, you know.'

'Of course you are, Adrian.' She rose from the bed, and opened the window curtains without waiting for a servant, letting the light stream in on them. 'But it is a beautiful morning. And to walk in the park, for just a little while, would be delightful.'

'You should not go out without escort,' he said absently, wondering if she meant to take a maid with them as well.

'I will have you.'

'You will not.'

'Just a short outing together. In sunlight.'

'Do you wish for me to ride in Rotten Row?' he snapped, wishing that he had not just revealed the fear he felt when he thought of so public a place. 'I suspect that would be most amusing for all concerned.'

'Of course I do not wish you to ride. If you mean to break your neck, then I pray you, find another way. You cannot trust a horse to do the deed without undo suffering. To me especially, for I would not wish to watch.'

And now she had made him laugh, against his better judgement.

'But there is nothing wrong with your legs, is there?' She had come back to the bed and her fingers were stroking them, with faint touches meant to raise the hairs and tease the nerves to restlessness.

He pulled away from her and sat up, dangling his feet off the edge of her bed. 'No.'

'How long has it been since you have enjoyed a simple walk in the park? You prowl the streets at night, of course. But it would be nice to feel the sun on one's face.' She crawled after him, putting her arms about his waist and giving a little squeeze. 'For both of us.'

She was right, of course. It must be difficult for her to meet only at night. While the secrecy was necessary, it must make her feel as though he was ashamed of her company. And he knew how sensitive she still was on the subject of her worth. 'It is not just a matter of revealing ourselves, my dear. I have not made my condition publicly known. And while it is possible to disguise it in familiar territory and for short periods of time, should I be seen blundering into a tree in Hyde Park, I suspect that the world will be too soon completely aware.'

'I am suggesting nothing of the kind,' she argued. 'It is not fashionable there until late in the afternoon. If we go now, no one will be about. We could keep our stroll short, on a path that is straight and level and far away from Kings Road. If you take my arm, you might lead me, and I will inform you of any obstacles, just as we do here. It will be most uneventful.'

'And not particularly interesting. If you wish to spend the day with me, I can think of better uses for your time.' He leaned against her, feeling her breasts pressing into his back, and her breath upon his neck.

'If a morning outing bores you, then you need have nothing to fear from it,' she responded tartly.

'Fear? I faced Napoleon's army without flinching. I do not avoid the park because I am afraid.' *Terrified* was more the word.

'Of course you are not. But I do not see why you cannot give me what I ask, when it is such a small thing.'

'It is because it's so small that I see no value in it.' He reached behind him to touch her face. 'Perhaps I could buy you a trinket. Some fobs for those lovely ears...'

'And how would I explain them to my friends? Would I tell them that my husband had given me a gift?' Now it was her turn to laugh bitterly. 'They will assume that I am unfaithful far more quickly from that than if they see me taking the air with a male acquaintance.'

She was glib this morning, and as frank as she had been from the first. But last night she had said she loved him. And he was pretending she had said nothing, and treating her little better than a whore, kept for one purpose, and plied with jewellery to avert a sulk. He shamed himself with his behaviour more than he ever could by groping his way around Hyde Park.

As if she could sense his weakening, she said, more softly, 'We will not be out for long. And tonight, for your reward, you can do as you like with me.' She was kissing his back now, and spreading her hands in his lap over his manhood, perfectly still as though waiting for his instructions. 'But for now? You owe me this, at least.'

Because you will not love me. That was what she meant, he was sure. And he wondered if this would be the first of many such bargains: pouts and capitulations that would lead to arguments, bitterness and regrets. If it was, it was likely the beginning of the end for them. The scales that had been so delicately balanced would never be right again. Last night, words had been spoken and they could not be unsaid.

But he did not want to give her up. Not yet. It was too soon. And although he had not intended to feel anything, ever again, she made him happy. He captured her hands before she could arouse him, and turned his face to kiss her, then pretended to consider. 'To do as I like with you? That is an offer I have no power to resist. Even without it, I will go. I need no other reason but that it pleases you. Now if you mean for me to leave this room in daylight, you had best let me dress before I change my mind and take you back to bed.'

Emily could see, from the moment they left the carriage, that the trip had been a good idea. She allowed the coachman to help her down, and then took her husband's arm as he waited on the ground for her. Adrian's face was tipped towards the sunlight; he was staring up into the canopy of leaves above them as though he had never seen such a wonderful thing.

Without knowing it, she would never have guessed that the sense of wonder had less to do with the fine day than his inability to see the trees with any clarity.

He looked down and to the side again, as he always did, tipping the brim of his hat a bit to provide more shade. 'There are tinted glasses they gave me, after the injury on the battlefield, to shield my eyes against the glare of the sun. Perhaps I shall find them again, for occasions like this.'

'You mean to go out with me again?'

He sighed. 'With or without you. Someday, rumour of my condition is bound to get out. There will be no point in hiding in my rooms when it does.'

It was the first she had heard of him planning for anything but his premature death. She stifled the surprise she felt, fearing that an acknowledgement of it might scare the idea from his head.

But he did not seem to notice his own change in attitude, and touched his own eyes thoughtfully. 'It might make it easier to manage in sunlight, with what vision I have left. And disguise any unfortunate staring on my part. I would not want to be thought rude.'

'An interesting sentiment, coming from the man I met a few days ago,' she answered.

He laughed again. 'No gentleman wishes to be met by

a lady in such surroundings as you found me. It makes it too difficult to pretend to any gentility at a later date. Come, let us take a turn around the park, so that I might prove I have manners.'

She gave his elbow a little squeeze. 'The path is just to the left. And straight on. There is no one in sight.'

'There never is, my dear.'

She cringed at her own insensitivity. 'I am sorry.'

'Why ever for? You did not strike me blind with your beauty,' he said, taking her hand and raising it to his lips for a salute. 'Nor do I begrudge you your vision.'

She relaxed a little as he put her hand back on his arm. 'Sometimes, I am still unsure how to behave around you. You have been angry enough to destroy your life over this, you know. It does not bespeak a man content in his disability.'

'Perhaps not. But today, things are different.' He took a deep breath. 'It is much harder to be bitter when the sun is shining and the roses are in bloom.'

'You can smell them?'

'You cannot?'

Emily paused and sniffed. Of course she could. But she had been far too focused on the delicate colour of them to notice the fragrance. She let him walk her closer to the bank of carefully tended flowers. 'They are beautiful,' she said.

'There was a fine garden of them at my home in Derbyshire. York and Lancaster and white damask, with boxwood hedges. I wonder if it is still there.'

Yes. We will walk in it yet this summer, my love. 'I

would expect so,' she said. 'A country home is nothing without a rose garden.'

'Describe these to me.'

'Red, pink, yellow.' It was quite inadequate to his needs, she was sure. 'The red has a touch of purple in it. And shadows. Like velvet in candlelight.'

He reached out a hand, and she put it on a bloom. 'The texture is velvet as well. Feel.'

She touched them, too, and found that he was right, then moved to the next bush. 'And these,' she said, 'are apple roses. Big and pink, and the velvet is more in the leaves than the flowers. And here are your damasks.'

He gave a nod of approval. 'As there should be.' And then he cocked his head. 'And there is a lark.'

She glanced around her. 'Where? I do not see him.'

He pointed, unerringly, towards a tree on their left. When she looked closely, she thought she saw a flash of feathers in the leaves. 'Poor confused fellow,' he said. 'It is past nesting season. Unusual to hear that particular song so late in the year.'

'They have different songs?'

'They speak to each other, just as we do.' He smiled, listening again. 'That is a male, looking for a mate.'

There was an answering warble, in a tree on the right. 'And there she is.' He sighed. 'He has found her after all. Well done, sir.' And, almost absently, he patted her arm.

She smiled up at him, happy to be in her rightful place, on the arm of the handsome Earl of Folbroke, even if it was just for an hour. She had never noticed the park to be so full of life before. But Adrian was quick to discover things that she had not noticed and to point them out to her as they passed. The few people that they met as they walked smiled and nodded, taking no more notice of her husband than they would have in any other passer-by.

She could feel him tense each time, as though fearing a response. And each time, when none came, he relaxed a bit more. 'There are more people here than you promised,' he said absently.

'I might have lied a bit in calling it empty. But it is not crowded. And not as bad as you feared, I am sure,' she said. 'I see no one that I recognise. And the people that are out take no notice of us, walking together. There is nothing so unique in your behaviour as to incite comment from a casual observer. In truth, we are a most unexceptional pair.'

He chuckled. 'My pride is well checked, madam. I have made an appearance in public and the sky did not fall. In fact, no one noticed. If they thought anything about me, I am sure they whisper at what a lucky fellow I am, to be taking the air with such a beauty.'

'You are in excellent spirits today.'

Adrian looked up, and around him, as though he could still see his surroundings. 'It is a beautiful day, is it not? You were right for forcing me into the sunlight, my dear. It has been far too long.'

'It has,' she said softly back to him. 'And I have another gift for you, if you will accept it from me.'

'It is not another piano, is it? Or perhaps some other musical instrument? Are you about to pull a trumpet from your reticule and force me to blow it and scare away the birds?'

'Nothing so great as that, I assure you.'

He smiled down at his feet. 'And it is not your own sweet person that you offer. Although if you were to suggest that we nip behind a rosebush for a kiss, I would not deny you.'

She gave him the mildest of rebukes, nudging his arm with her shoulder 'Not that, either.'

'Then I have no idea what you are about. But since we are in public when you offer it, I assume you are unsure of my reaction. Here you know I do not wish to call attention to myself, and will have little choice to accept, with grace, whatever you offer me.' There was a sardonic twist to his lip. 'Out with it. You are making me apprehensive.'

She reached into her reticule, digging for the card she had found. 'Can you read French?'

He gave her a dubious grin. 'Madam, I thought I made it plain enough the night we met that reading of any kind is quite beyond me.'

She responded with a sniff so that he might know of her annoyance, and said, 'You are being difficult with me again. And I am not being clear enough with you. For that, I apologise. I should have more rightly said, before your difficulty overtook you, did you learn to read the French language?'

It was his turn to huff impatiently at her. 'Of course I did. Despite what you might think, after finding me in such low estates, I was brought up properly and well educated. It might have been easier had I not been. One cannot miss what one has never known.'

'But you were fluent?'

'Better in Greek and Latin. But, yes, I managed tolerably well in French. I could understand and be understood. But I fail to see how that matters.'

Emily thrust the stiff sheet of paperboard into one of his hands, and placed the fingers of his other on the raised letters there. 'See what you can make of this.'

He frowned as he dragged his fingers over the surface, moving too quickly to interpret the patterns. 'What is it?' he whispered.

'A poem. The author was a Frenchman, and a scholar. And blind,' she added. 'From what I have been able to gather on the subject, the French people seem much more enlightened in the education of those with your problem. There are quite interesting experiments in place for the teaching of mathematics, geography and even reading and writing. But much of the work is all in French, and I have not...'

He held the card loosely, not even trying to examine it. 'And if you have not noticed, my love, we are currently at war with France.'

'But we will not be for ever. Once we have conquered Napoleon, there will be peace between our countries. I am sure of it. And then, perhaps, we might go to Paris.'

'And perhaps they will have established a language for me, and perhaps I shall learn it. And we will live together, in a little flat on the banks of the Seine, and forget our spouses and our common English troubles.

And I will write French poems to you.' He handed it back to her.

'Perhaps we shall.' She took the card and turned to him, forcing it into the pocket where he kept her picture. 'Although I understand the impossibility of some of what you are saying, is it really such a strange idea that you might be able to better yourself, or to live very much as other men do?'

He sighed, as though tired of arguing with her. 'You do not understand.'

'But I am trying to,' she said, 'which is more than your family taught you to do. When faced with the same challenge, your father and grandfather gave up. And they taught you to do the same.' She held his arm again, wrapping her fingers tightly around the crook of his elbow. 'But you are not like them. You are so much more than they were. And you will not know, until you have tried for yourself, what you are capable of. If you do not see that, then you are crippled with something far worse than blindness. You suffer from a lack of vision.'

Adrian stood still, as unresponsive as a mannequin. For a moment, she hoped that he was thinking about her words. And then he said in a gruff, irritable voice, 'Are you quite finished? Or do you have other opinions that you wish to share with me?'

'That is enough for the morning, I think.' She let out her held breath slowly, hoping that he did not notice, but was sure that he had, for he could read her like a book.

'I quite agree. I think it is time for me to escort you back to the carriage, if you will tell me where it is.'

She was in no mood to help him, fairly sure that he knew perfectly well where to go and was only feigning a need for instruction. 'The carriage has not moved since we left it. Take us back the way we came.'

There was a miniscule pause as he retraced his steps in his mind. Then he turned and led her back down the path that they had walked, feeling along the grassy edge of it with his stick to help him find the way.

They went along without incident, not speaking. She forced herself to stay relaxed at his side, praying that there would be no familiar faces amongst the few strollers there. She had half hoped, when they stood happily by the roses, that they would see some members of their set and engage them in a brief conversation, to gently reveal her true identity to her husband. But after the fresh start they had made this morning, she had overstepped herself. The distance born between them last night was growing. And if she could not find a way to stop it, she would lose him. She doubted it would be a pleasant experience for anyone should he be hailed by a friend and forced, without warning, to explain his condition.

They were within steps of the carriage, now, and she knew by the relaxing of the muscles in his arm that he knew it as well. While they walked, she had felt him tensing as he listened for clues, alert to any change, but now he had heard the jingle of the harnesses, and the chatter of the driver and grooms, silencing to attention as they drew near. He'd released her arm, putting a protective hand upon her back as she moved to step up and into it, when a call came from behind him.

'Alms!'

Adrian froze for a moment, as though the single word had the power to control him. Then he turned back, his head tracking to find the source.

'Alms for a blind beggar! Alms!' There was a woman beside the entrance to the park, probably hoping to catch some member of the *ton* on their way in or out. She stared towards them with eyes clouded milk-white, with no idea who she accosted, other than that they had sufficient funds to afford a carriage and should be able to spare a few pennies for her. When she shook the cup in her hand, it gave off the pathetic rattle of an unsuccessful morning.

Emily could feel the fingers on her back sliding away, as her husband turned, forgetting why he touched her. And she turned with him, taking her foot off the step and waving the groom away. She caught at Adrian, her fingers tightening on his arm, and he reached up with his other hand to grip them. It was not the gentle and reassuring touch she had grown accustomed to, but a rigid, claw-like reflex.

She tugged at his arm, trying to get him to move. 'Come, Adrian. We can go back to the carriage, if you like.'

Then his grip began to relax again, and he led her towards the woman, and not away. 'Tell me what you see. Spare no detail.'

'She is an old woman,' Emily said. 'Her clothes are

clean and in good repair, but they are simple. There are worn patches at the elbows, and the lace at the throat will not see many more washings. Her eyes were blue, but are obscured by pearls. Cataracts, I think they are sometimes called. I doubt she has been blind her whole life.'

As she spoke, the woman before them stood mute, accepting the scrutiny as though she had given up being anything more than an object of pity. And then her hand tightened on her cup and she gave it another little shake.

'Is this an accurate description?' he said. When he got no response, he fumbled to touch the beggar on the arm.

The woman started and shook his hand away, unsure of the reason for contact and frightened by it.

'I need to ask, because I am blind as well,' he said, in a soft and reassuring voice.

'Yes, sir.' The old woman gave a relieved smile.

'My lord,' Adrian corrected absently, reaching in his pocket for his purse. 'I am the Earl of Folbroke.'

The woman dropped into a curtsy.

And feeling the movement in her arm, he dipped his head in response to the gesture of respect. 'What brings you to this, old mother? Do you have no one to care for you?'

'My husband is dead,' she said. Her accent was not refined, but neither was it coarse. 'And my son is gone off to war. For a time, he sent money. But it has been long since I've heard anything. And I fear…' She stopped, as though she did not wish to think of what news was likely to come.

'It might mean nothing,' he assured her. 'I served as well. It is not always easy to get word home. But perhaps I can discover something. Today, I am busy. But tomorrow, you will come to my rooms in Jermyn Street. I will tell the servants to look out for you. And I will take your information and see if anything can be done with it.'

'Thank you, my lord.' The woman was near to breathless with shock, already. But when she heard him drop a coin into the cup, it was clear that she could tell the difference between gold and copper by the sound. Her surprised mouth closed, and widened in a smile. 'Thank you, my lord,' she said with more emphasis.

'Until tomorrow,' he said, and turned away from her, signalling the coachman for assistance with a whistle and a tap of his cane.

They rode in silence toward his rooms, until she could stand it no longer. 'That was a wonderful thing you did for her.'

'Soldiers have enough to worry about on the battlefield, without coming home to find that their mothers are begging in the streets,' he said, as though that was the only thing that concerned him. And then, as an afterthought, added, 'What I did was not enough. If there is a way to find honest employment for her, it will be done.'

There was a lump rising in her throat as they pulled to a stop before the building that housed his rooms. And as he rose to exit, she touched his arm to make him pause.

He turned his head, waiting for some word from her.

'I know you do not want to hear it. But I cannot help but speak,' she said. 'I love you, Adrian Longesley.'

He swallowed. Then he said, 'Thank you.' And then he left her, tapping his way to the steps of his door.

Chapter Fifteen

*T*hank you.

What an idiotic thing to say to a woman who had just bared her soul to him. But what else could he say to her? The response she wanted was not the one he wished to give her. And anything else seemed inadequate.

'Hendricks!' Adrian handed his hat and gloves to the footman and went directly to his room, hearing the secretary fall into step behind him.

'My lord?' Hendricks said, the words muffled by what was probably a mouthful of his breakfast.

'What time is it?'

'Half past eight. Very early for you, my lord.' This seemed to be not a reproof, but as an apology for his own lack of preparation.

'Very early for any coherence, you mean. Well, prepare to be surprised. Not only am I sober, but I have slept, breakfasted and gone for a walk.'

There was a little cough from behind him, as Hendricks inhaled a toast crumb from the shock.

Adrian smiled to himself. 'I am getting ahead of you today, it seems. Go, finish your breakfast. Or, if you wish, bring it to my room, along with the paper. You are welcome to use the table by the window, if you wish. The breeze this morning is particularly nice. And the view, from what I can gather, is quite pleasant.'

'Thank you, my lord.'

His valet had preceded him and was waiting in the bedroom to take his coat, making every effort not to appear as flat footed as Hendricks. As it slid from his shoulders, Adrian reached, as he always did, for the miniature in the breast pocket.

His fingers brushed something unexpected. It was a moment before he remembered the bit of card that had been forced on him in the park.

He balled his fist in frustration, then quickly relaxed it so as not to crush the paper. He had not handled that well. He should not have laughed at her attempts to help him, or snapped. It would be all his loss if she left him after one of those outbursts of temper.

Especially when fate had then demonstrated just how small his problems were in comparison to others. Perhaps his lover was wrong and he had reached the end of his usefulness. Perhaps he would spend the rest of his life sitting in the window, listening to the world pass by. But at least he would not be forced to spend it on a corner with a tin cup.

The image in his mind of such a common thing, a

future in Paris, or anywhere else, with his lover sprawled close to him on a *chaise* while they drank wine and read poetry to each other, had been sharp and painful. The idea that there could be any permanence in what they had seemed as unattainable as if she'd told him they would fly to the moon.

As he sat to be shaved, he fingered the card in his hands, tracing the rows of pinpricks with his nail. If he'd simply attempted to read the thing while she was there, she'd have seen how hopeless it was, and she'd have given up bothering him with it.

Or he'd have proved her right. His pride must be a very fragile thing, if he feared success as much as failure. He ran his fingers over the surface of the card, noting that the bumps were set in patches, and the patches in rows. And when he forced himself to move very slowly, he could begin to make out letters.

She was right. It seemed to be in French. He chuckled, as he began to understand the words, wondering if she had attempted them herself. How hard could it have been to read them, if one was able to make out the embossing on the page?

"'Love is both blind itself and makes all blind whom it rules,'" he read aloud, and heard the valet grunt in irritation and give a stern warning of 'my lord' against sudden movement while at the mercy of a man with a razor.

Adrian smiled cautiously to prevent injury and thought of the woman who had given him the card. It was very like her to choose these as the first words he had read in months. For a moment, he thought it might be Shakespeare, and nothing more than an ironic choice on her part. But she had been wrong about the contents being poetry. It seemed that the man was not a poet at all, but a Latin scholar, and a blind one as well.

He traced his fingers over the letters again, faster this time, as they grew more fluent with the feel of what he found there. Still not as fast as if he could read. But it felt good to recognise the ideas forming under his hand. The writer had called blindness a divine good, rather than a human ill. The idea made Adrian smirk, causing another groan from his valet. If the Almighty had smitten the Folbrokes in an attempt to make them divine messengers of goodness, then God must be blind as well. Choosing such an unworthy lot did not bespeak much for His taste in servants.

And yet…

'Hendricks.'

'Lord Folbroke.' His secretary, who had settled at the little table by the window, answered in a voice clear of any obstruction.

'Can you recall—has there ever been a Member of Parliament who was struck blind?'

'Of course, my lord.'

Adrian leaned forwards hopefully, only to hear, 'You, my lord. And your father, of course. And grandfather.'

'No, you ninny. Someone from another family.'

'None that I know of, my lord. But certainly it is not impossible. There are those that are lame, aren't there?'

'And deaf, as well. And probably without sense,'

Adrian added. 'For how else can we justify the decisions that are made by them?'

'I can look into it, if you wish. But I suspect that they would have little choice but to make accommodations for…any peer that was so inconvenienced.'

Good old Hendricks. He had been about to say *you*—and had taken care to stop himself, lest he be guilty of putting words in my lord's mouth. 'Please, do. And let me know what you discover. I have another task for you as well. I need to speak with someone in the Horse Guards to see if there is anything to be done about locating the fate of a soldier. I met the man's mother in the park today…'

'In the park,' Hendricks parroted, as though he could not quite believe what he had heard.

'Just outside of it, actually. Circumstances had reduced her to begging in the street. And I said that I would attempt to help her, if she came to my rooms tomorrow.'

'A beggar is coming here, my lord?'

'Yes, Hendricks. A blind beggar. She is the mother of a soldier.'

'I see, my lord.'

'And whether the news is good or bad, if some sort of pension could be arranged for her…'

'Consider it done, my lord.' Hendricks set down his cup and rose from his chair, ready to begin his errands. 'Is there anything else?' The last was said as though he assumed dismissal was imminent.

'Actually, there is.' As the secretary neared him,

Adrian passed him the card he had been holding. 'What do you make of this?'

'It is a lecture by Jean Passerat, my lord.'

'I am aware of that, Hendricks. Because I read it.'

'My lord.' The exclamation was so surprised that Adrian suspected it was a hushed prayer and not meant for him at all.

'You can see how the letters are raised up. I can feel them, Hendricks. It is a laborious process, to read these pinpricks, but not impossible. And it occurs to me that there might be a stationer or a printer who could do something similar. They have the raised lead type already in their possession.'

Hendricks thought for a moment. 'That is backwards, to make the impression on the page.'

'But if they could make a mould, somehow. Or if special letters were struck that were the right way round.' Adrian drummed his fingers on his knee, imagining all the ways that such a system could be applied. And suddenly he felt eager to be up and doing something. 'It would be expensive, I suppose. But I have the money.'

'You do indeed, my lord.' Hendricks sounded relieved, now. And happy.

'And if it can be done for me, then I see no reason why other reading materials cannot be made. Perhaps the Southwark Asylum could take some on. I know they do not think it is their place to educate the residents, but I beg to differ on the subject.'

'And who would know better than you, my lord? You have a very personal interest in the subject.'

'Which would put me in an excellent position to become a patron of that institution, I am sure. The combination of money and influence could be instrumental in making a long-lasting change in the place.'

'Of course, for the residents to feel the full benefits of your assistance, a considerable amount of time might need to be devoted to the subject,' Hendricks cautioned.

Time. And when had he not had enough of it? Days stretched on before him, and the rush to dull the ennui had been at the base of so many of his diversions. Adrian smiled. 'It seems to me, Hendricks, that of all the mad endeavours of my family, in three generations, the support of a charity has not been on the list. By the traditional standards of the house of Folbroke, I shall be behaving quite recklessly should I rush in any direction other than my own doom.'

'Very true, my lord.' There was definite amusement in the voice of his servant. 'You could very well be the wildest of your family, if you mean to squander your estate in philanthropy.'

'It would give me a chance to appreciate your dry wit, Hendricks. It is a quality I have missed in our recent interactions.'

'Of late you have given me little reason for mirth, Lord Folbroke.'

'Change is in the air, Hendricks. I am my old self, again, after a very long time.'

'So it would seem, my lord.'

'Can you not manage, after all the time in my service, to call me Adrian? Or Folbroke, at least.'

'No, my lord.' But the title was given with affection, and so he allowed it to pass. Hendricks cleared his throat. 'But if I might take the liberty of informing Lady Folbroke of your improved mood, she might be most gratified.'

Adrian felt the return of the old panic at the realisation that Emily would get wind of his plans, should they be carried too far before he had explained himself. 'That must wait until I have had a chance to speak to her myself. But you think she would approve?'

'Yes, my lord. She still enquires after you regularly. And she has been concerned by your silence.'

'But she did not respond to my summons.'

'If I might be so bold, my lord, as to offer advice?'

'Of course.'

'I believe it was the manner, and not the man, she objected to.'

Adrian sighed. 'I have made so many mistakes with the poor girl I hardly know where to begin to rectify them.'

'She has not been a poor girl for some time, my lord.' And there again was that strange sense of admiration that he heard sometimes when Hendricks spoke to him of his wife. And he remembered that the reconciliation he imagined might not be welcomed by his friend.

'It is my own punishment that I was not there to see Emily blossom into the woman she has become. Too proud to watch her with half my sight. And now I cannot see her at all.' He sighed. 'Thank you for taking care of her, Hendricks.'

'I? I have done nothing, my lord.'

'I suspect that is not true.' And what did he expect the man to say? Nothing he wanted to hear. But Adrian could not seem to leave the subject alone.

Hendricks said, after some thought, 'For the most, she takes care of herself. I do very little but to follow her wishes. But I am sure, if you speak to her for yourself, you will find her eager to listen.'

'Perhaps I shall.' And his nerve failed him again. 'But not today. Today, I think I shall go out for lunch.'

'Out, my lord?' He could almost hear Hendricks's brain, ticking through the possibilities, trying to decide where he would be drawn so early in the day. And whether there would be a way from dissuading him from whatever fresh folly he had discovered. For though the morning had been full of promise, Adrian had given his poor friend no reason to believe that his good intentions would last to the afternoon.

When Hendricks could not come up with the answer on his own, he responded, 'When I have completed the tasks you set for me, I will accompany you.'

'Will you, now? And did I ask for a companion, Mr Hendricks?'

'No, my lord.'

'Then you needn't stir yourself. What I do, I must do for myself. You are not a member, after all.'

'Not a member? What the devil…?' For a moment, Hendricks was completely lost. And his subservience slipped, revealing the man underneath.

Adrian reached out into the open air, until he could

find the secretary's arm and give it a reassuring pat. 'Do not concern yourself, man. I am not an infant. I will manage well enough on my own for a few hours in broad daylight. Now, call for the carriage. And tell the cook I will not be home for supper.'

White's.

It was the very bastion of the sort of gentlemanly society that he had denied himself in the months since his sight had utterly failed. He had forgotten how peaceful it was, compared to the taverns he had been frequenting, and the sense of belonging and entitlement that a membership carried with it. It was a place where eccentricity was ignored. If a man had the blunt and the connections to be invited through the front door, then even aberrant behaviour might be deemed, if not creditable, at least not worthy of comment.

And when comment could no longer be restrained, then someone would most likely get out the betting book. Adrian grinned in anticipation.

'Lord Folbroke. May I help you with your hat and coat?'

'You can help me with several things,' he said, turning to the servant and placing his hand on the man's arm. 'It has been some time since I have been here. Have the arrangements changed at all?'

'My lord?' The footman seemed surprised, and a little confused at the question.

'It is my eyes, you see.' He passed his own hand in front of his face, to indicate the imperviousness of them.

'Not as blind as a bat, perhaps. But near enough.' *Blind.* Saying the word aloud felt good, as though it had been trapped on his tongue for an age, waiting to be shaken off. 'Take my hat and gloves. But my stick must remain with me.' Then he added, 'And I would appreciate a brief description of the room and its occupants.'

Once he was aware of what was required, the servant was totally amenable to the task, and not the least bit shocked or embarrassed by the request. He explained, *sotto voce,* who and what were to be found on the other side of the threshold. Then he said, 'Will there be anything else, my lord?'

'A drink, perhaps. Whatever the others are enjoying. You may bring it to me, once I have found a seat. And please announce yourself when you do so, for I might not hear you approach.' Then he turned back to the difficult task of re-entering society.

He stood for just a moment, taking a deep breath of the familiarly stuffy air. It was a trifle too hot in the room for him. But hadn't it always been so? He could smell alcohol and tobacco. But not the foul stuff he'd grown accustomed to. The smell of quality was as sharp as the ink on a fresh pound note.

'Folbroke!' There was a cry of welcome at the sight of him, followed by the sudden silence as his old friends realised that something had changed.

'Anneslea?' He started forwards, towards the voice of his old friend Harry and forgot himself, stumbling into a table and almost upsetting a game of cards. He apologised to the gentlemen in front of him, and turned to go around, only to feel Harry seize him by the arm and draw him forwards.

'Folbroke. Adrian. It has been almost a year since I have seen you. Where have you been?' And then a quieter, and more worried, 'And what has happened? Come. Sit. Talk.'

He smiled and shrugged, allowing the help of friendship. 'I have not been very good company, I am afraid.' Anneslea pressed him to a chair, and almost instantly the servant returned with a glass of wine. Adrian took a sip to steady his nerves. Suddenly, speaking a few simple words seemed more fearsome than a cavalry charge. 'My eyes failed me.'

'You are…?'

'Blind.' He said it again, and again there came a small lightening of spirit. 'It has been all downhill since that flash burn in Salamanca.'

Harry gripped his arm. 'There is no hope for recovery?'

Adrian patted his hand. 'The eyes in my family are no damned good at all, I'm afraid. The same thing happened to my father. I had hoped to dodge the condition. But it appears I am not to be spared.'

There was the pause he'd expected. Then Anneslea burst forth with a relieved laugh. 'Better to find you blind than foxed before noon. When I saw you running into the furniture, I feared I'd have to take you home and put you to bed.'

The men around him laughed as well, and for a change he laughed with them, at his own folly.

'Folbroke?'

Adrian offered a silent prayer for strength. 'Rupert. How good to see you.'

'But you just said, you cannot see me.'

Some things had not changed. He still enjoyed the company at White's—except for the days when his cousin was present. 'I was speaking metaphorically, Rupert.' *As I was when I said it was good to see you.* 'Although you are not visible to me—' *and that is a blessing* '—you can see that I have no trouble recognising you by your voice.'

'Your other faculties are not impaired?' Rupert sounded almost hopeful to be proven wrong. Could the man not pretend, even for an instant, that he was not waiting in the wings to snatch the title away?

'No, Rupert,' he said as patiently as possible. 'You will find that I am still quite sharp. And since my brief period of reclusion is nearing its end, I will be returning to my usual haunts, and my place in the Parliament.'

'And I suppose Lady Folbroke spoke the truth as well?'

About what? he wondered. And then decided to give his wife the benefit of the doubt. 'Of course. She would have no reason to lie, would she?'

'I suppose not. But then, congratulations are in order,' Rupert said glumly.

'Congratulations, old man?' Anneslea addressed this to him. 'You come to me with your dead eyes, and nothing but bad news. But your wife spreads the glad tidings, I suppose. What is it that we are celebrating?'

Not a clue. 'I will let Rupert tell you, since he is obviously eager to share what he has learned.'

Rupert gave a sigh, sounding as far from eager as it was possible to be. 'It seems that there will be a new heir to Folbroke, by Easter.'

Chapter Sixteen

When Hendricks came to her that afternoon with news of his errands, Emily could barely contain her excitement. It seemed the blind beggar had done more in the space of a few moments than she had managed in a week. 'He saw himself in her, I am sure. And has been reminded of the advantages of his rank. Thank you so much, for helping to lead him the rest of the way.' She leaned forward and clutched Hendricks by the arm, as he sat taking tea with her, so overcome with emotion at the thought of a brighter future that she thought she would burst from happiness.

At her touch, Hendricks gave a start that rattled his saucer, and glanced down at her hand as though he did not know quite what to do about it. 'You give yourself too little credit, Lady Folbroke. It is your devotion to him that made the difference.'

'And did he say anything of me?' she asked hopefully.

'Emily, that is. His wife.' And she began to realise the extent of her confusion. It was as if she was two people, and unsure which of them would deserve Adrian's attention.

'I asked if I should go to you with this news. And he acknowledged that you would need to hear of it sooner, rather than later, and that he wished to speak to you himself. You will have some contact from him in the next day or so. I am sure of it.'

'That is good,' she said, closing her eyes in a silent prayer of thanks.

'Perhaps his outing this afternoon will shed more light upon his plans.'

'An outing?' This was news, but she could not tell whether it was good or bad. 'Did he say where he was going? Or when he might return? And who accompanied him?' She peppered Hendricks with questions, until the poor man held up a hand to stop her.

'He would not tell me, nor would he accept my escort. He left word that he would not be dining at home. But I assume he means to return long enough to dress and then visit you here, this evening. Beyond that, I know no more than you.'

'That leaves me nothing to do but wait,' she said, getting up to pace the room. 'I did not give two thoughts to the risks he was taking, for all the time he was gone. I just assumed that he would be well.'

'And he managed well without your help,' Hendricks reminded her.

'It is not as if I do not trust him to take care of himself,' she said, trying to convince herself that it was a fact. 'But now that I have seen him, and know how reckless he can be—' she looked desperately at Hendricks '—what shall I do? What shall I do if he does not come back?' When she had come to London, she had been worried about household economies and the loss of her freedom. But now the thought consumed her that, if she should never see him again, it would mean that he would never know who she was, or how she felt for him.

Hendricks stared down into his teacup. 'Lord Folbroke would be most annoyed with me should I leave you to worry over nothing. You need have no fear for yourself, for even if the worst should occur, you are not without friends. You will not be alone, Emily. You shall never be alone.'

'But I have no thought for myself,' she said, going to look out the window in the vain hope that she would see his carriage pass by. 'It is only he that I care about. He is at the centre of all my happiness. And now that I have found him again, I must keep him safe and healthy, and happy as well. Just as he was this morning.'

'Then you must trust him,' Hendricks said. 'In a few hours, all will be right again. You will see.'

At a little before eight o'clock, she heard the sound of Adrian's step in the hall and his call for a servant to take his hat and gloves. She rushed past the footman, dismissing the servant so that she could tend to him herself, running into his arms and pressing a kiss upon his lips.

Tonight, though well dressed, Adrian was not his usual, immaculate self. His cravat was tied loosely, his brown hair was mussed, and there was colour in his cheeks as though he had just come back from a ride, or some other strenuous pursuit. He gave a laugh when he recognised the feel of her, and gathered her close in a kiss so hungry that it bordered on violence.

He tasted of brandy, and salt as well. She felt a strange wetness upon her own lips. When she managed to push him clear so she could wipe it away, there was red on her fingers. She reached out gently to touch his mouth, and he flinched and batted her hand away. 'There is a cut on your lip.'

It was odd. For instead of the reaction she had been expecting, of a curse or another wince of pain, he ran a finger tentatively across the wound and grinned at her, wolfish and wicked. 'So there is.'

She reached into her sleeve and withdrew a handkerchief, wetting it the tip of her tongue and reaching up to dab away the blood.

He pulled her close again, lifting her so that her toes barely touched the ground and gave a growl. 'Kiss it better?'

'I do not want to hurt you.'

''Tis a pity that the man who hit me did not feel the same. Of course, I'd pegged him good by the time he landed this on me. So I suppose I had it coming.' Her husband was still grinning, blue eyes sparkling with an emotion that she had not seen before. And he kissed her again, as he had on that first night, as though he could not wait to take her to bed and did not care who knew it.

'You were fighting?' The words and the kiss sent her thoughts rushing back to the man he had been when she'd found him. She sniffed his breath again. 'You have been drinking, haven't you?'

'And what if I have?' He kissed her throat, fondling her body through the gown she wore.

She pushed at his hands, trying to catch her breath. 'You promised me that there would be no more of that. You are too valuable to me to squander yourself. I was beside myself with worry over you.'

He paused, leaning his face against her hair. 'Really, madam, you cannot expect me to place my calendar totally in your hands, no matter how lovely those hands might be. My life is still my own, is it not?' But somehow, he did not sound particularly happy with his freedom.

'Of course it is,' she assured him. 'You know I have no claim on you. But no matter what happens between us, it is very important to me to know you are safe and well.'

He leaned against her for a moment, as though his day had exhausted his strength. 'And I thank you for it. It is good to know that someone cares. And you need have no fear of my condition. I gained it as any proper gentleman should. I went to White's for luncheon.'

'You went out again? And without me?' She could not control the little shriek of delight she gave and threw her arms about his neck.

He gave her a pat upon the shoulder and shrugged as though the sudden change was nothing unusual. 'I could not very well take you to my club, darling. No ladies allowed. Not even wives, thank God.' The last was uttered under his breath, so quiet that she barely heard it. And then he continued, as if he had said nothing. 'My taking lunch there should not be such an uncommon thing to you. I am still a member, in good standing. Anneslea was there, as was his brother-in-law, Tremaine. Good to see them again, after all this time. Anneslea asked about the eyes, of course.'

'And you told them?' She leaned away from him, staring into his face.

'Unlike some problems, my condition is rather hard to conceal.' He looked past her, not even pretending to see. Then he gave another non-committal shrug, as though his mind had moved on to other, far more important matters than the one thing that had consumed him for months.

She hugged him again and kissed him on his sore lip. 'But what of this?'

'After we got the niceties out of the way, there were others who were eager to share the news of the day with me. Some of which was quite surprising. It seems I have much reason to celebrate. My cousin Rupert was there...' He frowned again, pinching his lips tight together until the cut went white.

That might explain his strange mood. She doubted he had wanted to reveal himself so soon to his family.

And she knew from experience that Rupert had a way of ruining even the happiest of days.

Adrian seemed about to say something, and then smiled again, and went on with his story. 'In the course of the afternoon, the bottle was passed around. We got to talking about what was possible for a blind man to accomplish. And then, someone got out the betting book.' He gave another shrug, as though to minimise the foolishness of it. But it was coupled with a satisfied grin. 'Some of the fellows and I went off to Gentleman Jackson's for a bit of pugilism, as any proper gentleman of the *ton* might. Blindfolds for both men. Since I have the advantage of some sight, it would be hardly fair for me to go without. When equally blinded, it seems that I can manage two out of three opponents. A healthy average, I think. I proved quite good at finding my mark. If I can stay out of reach of the first few blows, I can hear the other fellow breathing like a bellows, and take aim upon the source of the sound. I am not as fast as I used to be, and my form was sadly lacking after this extended period of inactivity. But they could not fault my enthusiasm. Although it was a shame that the man I wanted to stand up with was not there to share the moment…'

'You boxed?' She did not know whether to laugh or scold him.

'Just a little harmless sparring. No anger behind it.' But the glittering of his eyes and the set of his jaw made her wonder at the truth of that. 'It was a shame that dear Rupert was too big a coward to share the ring. I dare say, after today's demonstration, he will not think me a helpless invalid, and will know to shut his mouth and keep his distance.'

And wasn't that what she had wanted all along? She gave him another enthusiastic kiss.

'You are glad that Anneslea split my lip?'

'I am glad that you left the house in daylight, and spent time in the company of true friends.' She stretched to kiss both of his damaged eyes. 'And that you told them.'

Adrian pressed his lips on the top of the head. 'It is your fault, you know, with your continual prodding that I do something with my life. And you were right. It was time. A little past time, I think.' And then he kissed her on the mouth. But although it started as a gentle kiss of thanks, it soon became something different.

His hat and gloves fell to the floor, and he gave them a kick that sent them across the hall, clear of their feet. Then his empty hands found her body, moving from her shoulders down her back, crushing her breasts to the front of his coat so he could feel them, and lower until she could feel the first stirrings of his erection pressing against her belly. Though his injured lips were soft on hers, his tongue moved in her mouth, rough and hungry. The brandied taste of it made her drunk with answering desire.

It would take little seducing to gain her ends tonight. He would make love to her, if she asked him to. For there was no sense of playfulness in his kiss, only the demand for swift release.

And as her body readied itself to succumb, her mind

whispered that more had changed than this. In the new world he was creating, there would be no place for secrets. And no way to hide his mystery lover from his friends, or his illness from his wife. Now that he had moved into the light, he was poised on the brink of yet another decision. And there was a chance that she might lose him for ever, if she did not talk soon and tell him everything. She broke from the kiss and freed herself from his grasp, then grabbed his arm and tugged. 'Come. You may tell me all about your plans, over dinner.'

'I have already eaten,' he said, pulling her back and running his hands over her bare arms.

'A glass of wine, then.'

He kissed her again, and said, 'You know what I want. And it is not food or wine. Do not deny me.' With one hand, he locked her hips to his, and with the other he pushed her breasts high, until they strained at the neckline of her bodice. Then he gave a yank on the fabric that covered them. She heard a button pop and her dress gaped. And he bent her back over his arm, and took her nipples in his mouth by turn, sucking hard upon them, biting them, leaving the exposed breast marked with his kisses, plain to see by anyone who might wander into the entranceway of the flat.

He was holding her so tightly that she had no breath to resist him. But the helplessness felt right. This was her husband, after all. And he was so overcome with desire for her that she doubted he'd have heard an objection, had she made one.

And then he paused, raising his head from her aching breasts. 'Last night, and this morning, when you said—'

'Let us pretend I said nothing.' She answered hurriedly, for she did not want him to stop again. 'Do not punish me for what I feel.'

'I do not mean to punish you. I only wish to be sure that your feelings have not changed.'

'They will never change,' she swore, panting, eager for him to resume. 'No matter what might happen between us, I will be steadfast.'

He seemed to flinch a little at this, as though he had hoped for some other answer. 'Good,' he said. 'Because otherwise, I would not...' And then it did not seem to matter, for he was kissing her again, undoing fastenings, pushing her dress farther down her body until he could stroke the tops of her hips above the fabric as he nibbled her shoulders. 'Say whatever you like. Nothing stands between us.'

She gasped, and said, 'I love you.'

He made no effort to answer with a similar sentiment. Instead, he said, 'Show me.' Then he pulled her, as sure as if he could see the way, through the sitting room and towards her bed.

She closed the door behind them. And before it was shut, he had pushed her gown to the floor and was tearing at his cravat to loosen the knot. When he tossed the fabric away and reached for the buttons of his vest, she stayed his hand. 'You will not be able to find things again, if you are so careless.'

He gave a strange laugh. 'Tonight, I am quite past caring.'

She stepped clear of her own clothing and kissed his bare throat. 'Then let me. I have watched you, these last nights. I will lay them out, just as you have. There will be no mistakes. But do not deny me the pleasure of undressing you.'

He gave a chuckle that was half sigh. Then he stood still, his arms a little apart from his body, as though he were standing for a valet. She felt a tremor go through his body at the first touch of her hands.

First, she took his coat, feeling the weight of her own picture and the purse in his pockets, and set it on the back of the chair. And then the waistcoat, and the cravat that she'd picked from the floor, one on top the other, folded and draped over the coat.

She paused to touch him. Broad shoulders, straight back, trim waist—she had seen him in bed, and touched every inch of him. But it had never been like this, with his body half-hidden by clothing. She pressed her lips to the opening at the throat of his shirt, spreading her fingers over the linen, feeling. Then she pushed the cloth out of the way and kissed his chest.

'You are a most interesting valet, madam,' he said, stroking her body before cupping his hand to the back of her neck and urging her to take his nipple into her mouth. 'A man could grow used to this.'

And she thought the same. He made her feel safe and cared for, even as he allowed her to care for him. And it was good to feel the hair on his chest brushing against her cheek, a hint of softness over muscles that were strong and sure. She stripped the shirt over his head, shook the wrinkles from it and laid it carefully with the cravat, then went back to him, rubbing her hands over his bare chest, before pushing him the few steps back to sit on the bed behind him. She sat on the floor to pull off his boots and stockings, stroking his calves, working her way up his legs and undoing buttons, pulling trousers aside and finding him fully awake to her touch.

She set the rest of his clothing by the chair. Then she went to the night table and doused the last candle so that they could lie in darkness.

As she did, he called out to her in surprise.

'Does it bother you to have no light?' she asked.

He reached to take her hand as she climbed up on to the bed with him. 'You will think me foolish, but I have a fear of the dark, when it comes on me suddenly. I am never sure if the last of my sight is leaving without warning, or it is merely a guttering candle.' He gave a nervous laugh. 'With the lights extinguished, we are both equally blind, are we not?'

'Yes,' she said, surprised that she had not thought of it. 'It will teach me to use my hands to find my way, as you do.'

'In darkness, we could be anyone. We could imagine anything. Fulfil our darkest wishes,' he whispered. 'And no one will see.' He kissed, long and hard, full of need, holding her so tight against his body as he did it that she could scarcely breathe. It was another proof of how easily he could dominate her, should he choose, and it made her shudder with anticipation. Then he relaxed back upon the bed to prove how utterly she had tamed him, giving her leave to explore him further, waiting to see what she would do with the freedom.

She straddled his legs, squeezing his thighs between hers and leaning forwards over him so that she could touch the muscles of his chest with her breasts. She could tell by his breathing that the faint touches of her nipples against his skin were as arousing to him as they were to her. He reached for them, pulling her breasts up and cupping them in his hands so that he could take them into his mouth again, rubbing them against the front of his teeth and nipping suddenly, then releasing them to blow them dry with his breath until they felt tight and cool.

She sat up and slid away from him again, running her hands down his abdomen, settling them upon his member and stroking it from base to tip, holding it against the skin of her belly in a way she knew he liked.

He let her work over him for a few moments before bringing his own hands down his body to meet hers, grasping her around the crease at the top of her thighs until his thumbs met between her legs, stroking her. 'Slowly,' he cautioned, while speeding up his own hands. 'Let me last. I want to enjoy you the whole of the night.' His hands came around her body, grasping her bottom. 'Slide forwards. Onto me. I want to be in you.'

She glanced at the chair across the darkened room, thinking one last time of the sheath in his pocket. 'Did you want…?'

'Do not think of it,' he commanded, as though he could guess her thoughts. Then he pulled her hips up his body so that he could rub himself against the wetness between her legs. 'This will be better. If you still wish it.'

'Yes,' she answered, guiding him even closer to where he belonged. She bent forwards and kissed him and rose up on her knees so she could touch herself with the tip of him, as though that were a kiss as well. Then she eased forwards, just an inch, and felt the beginnings of satisfaction as he began to slip inside.

'So good,' he whispered. 'But I want more.' He reached behind her again, trapping her hips and forcing her suddenly down and on to him in one quick, smooth stroke, until he filled her completely. 'There.'

She gasped in shock. She had forgotten how big he felt, resting inside her. And this sudden entrance was nothing like the cautious way he had thrust when he had last done this. Then he had seemed afraid to frighten her.

But tonight there was none of that. Before she could catch her breath, he was moving under her, into her. His hips rose and fell, bucking and grinding against hers as he sought release, making her tremble with excitement at the ease with which he controlled her body.

He slowed for a moment, seeming ready to withdraw. So she pressed against him again, guiding him farther, letting him slide deeper into her until she was sure that he would not change his mind. 'You did not want this from me, Adrian. What has changed?'

He groaned, but did not pull away. 'Am I hurting you?'

'No. It is so good. I want it.'

'Then nothing has changed. Say the words you said to me last night.'

'I love you, Adrian.' She tried to give an answering thrust, but he held her in place against his body. 'Take me. Please, Adrian, make love to me.'

'Yes. Again.' He sank into her, sighing in satisfaction. He was stroking slowly now, in and out of her, making her forget that it could be any way else.

'I love you.'

Then he slowed even more, skin sliding against skin, his hands on her back, moving to clutch her so that he could push with more force. She leaned forwards to lie on top of him. Suddenly, he rolled with her, over and onto her.

She dug her fingers into him, raking his back, afraid that he was trying to escape, and terrified that he would not finish what he had started.

And he laughed at her, as wicked as he had been that first night, straddling her as she had him and pumping hard into her until she lay breathless under him. She was close, so very close now, and he knew it. And he stopped to touch her face.

She nipped at his fingers, begging him to finish her, and he felt her eagerness and pulled his hand away and left her body.

She reached for him, flailing in desperation, and he grabbed her hands and rolled her onto her side. 'No, my darling,' he murmured. 'I will give you what you want, soon enough. You promised this morning that I would have whatever I liked from you. There are other ways to join. And tonight, I mean to try as many as I can.' He was entering her again, from behind, pushing up and down, and pressing hard against places inside her body that had barely felt him before. His hands were on her breasts now, circling the nipples as he thrust, his lips on her ear. 'Does this please you?' he growled, holding her tight.

'Yes,' she gasped, totally possessed by him, totally in his power.

'I am going to make you mine, soon,' he said close to her ear. 'And then I will do it again. And again. I will love you until there is nothing left in you but need of me. And then I will love you again.' He thrust harder and her climax began at the thought of having his seed inside her. And as she relaxed, satisfied that he would finally be hers, his hand came down to press between her legs and rub against her special place. He moved his thumb there in little flicks, keeping time with his thrusts until she broke again and again, mindless and helpless, shaking in his arms, crying his name.

And he felt her surrender and followed her, releasing deep inside her with a cry of 'Emily'.

The joy of it shot through her in a final spasm. He knew her. In this most intimate moment, without sight or words, he had recognised her.

Then he groaned and pulled away, shuddering and covering his face with his arm, as though he could hide himself from her by the act.

She rolled to lie close to him, wrapping an arm around

his waist and pulling at his hand until she could see the faint glitter of his eyes in the moonlight as he stared, sightless, towards the ceiling.

At last he spoke. 'I am sorry. I did not think. But I have saved myself for her for too long.'

'Your wife?' she asked softly.

'When I could not stand to be alone, and availed myself of the services of some nameless woman or other, it was her I imagined. Always her.'

He reached out to touch her hair. 'This week has been different, I swear it. But tonight, when it should have been no one but you, I used what you felt for me. I lied and pretended to be what you wanted me to be. And while I did it, I thought of her. I did not mean to say that name. You are precious to me. It would not have been thus, were you not. And I do not wish to hurt you.'

'It is all right,' she said, trying to gain understanding of what had just happened. The man beside her was racked with guilt over feeling just what she wanted him to feel for the woman he had left behind. She rolled even closer to lean over him and put her hands on his face, kissing his eyes and his lips, and whispering words of love. 'It is all right. It changes nothing between us. I understand. She is with you, even as my husband is never far from my thoughts.'

'She is in London. She will hear of my visit to White's. She will hear about my eyes.'

'Rumours, perhaps,' she answered. 'But it will be better if she hears the rest of it from you.'

'And I have heard things as well,' he whispered. 'But

not rumours. More truth than I ever wanted to know.' He pulled her down on top of him, into his arms, crushing her cheek to his chest and she could feel the pain in him in the vibrations as he spoke. 'She came to me, on the day we met. And I was not there for her. It would have been so much easier, had I been there when she needed me. And I failed her, because of my selfishness. It must not happen again.'

'Your words do you credit,' she said, glad that he could not see the smile on her face, for there was no way she could have explained it.

He must have caught some trace of her mood, for he said, a little puzzled, 'You understand what this will mean to us?' His voice was sad, but resolute. 'This cannot go on. I must go home to her.'

'I knew that what we shared could not last, as did you.' She gathered his hand to her mouth and kissed it lightly, in the dark, glad that he could not know how happy she felt. 'And I know that you love her. You cannot see it, of course. But on the day you showed me her picture, I knew. You have worn the paint away from the continual touching of it. You want to be with her. You know it is true.'

He gave a weak laugh. 'More than I understood. More than I ever believed possible. I can deny it no longer. The woman is my home, and all I could have hoped for, had my life been different. I wronged her horribly by keeping the truth from her. And I have waited too long. Things have been lost that can never be regained.'

'You will not know for sure until you speak to her,' she urged.

'I know it, true enough,' he said. 'About some things, there is nothing more that can be done. And now, I must make the best of what I have left.'

She touched his face again, wishing she could soothe his worries away and tell him how little the blindness mattered. 'It will be all right. But you must go to her.'

He laughed again. 'It is most unusual to accept advice from one's mistress on what to do about the deep and unrequited feelings one might bear for one's wife.'

'Your feelings are not unrequited.'

'How can you know?'

'Because I know you. And as I love you, so will she. If you let her.'

He pulled his hand away and wrapped his arms around her again, holding her close to him as though he were afraid to lose her. 'And then, what will become of you?'

'I will find my husband again, just as I planned to from the first.'

'He left you.'

'And yet I have never stopped loving him.'

He held her even tighter. 'I know it is wrong. And that I cannot have you. But I envy him even a portion of your affection, just as I long to be elsewhere. I am selfish and stupid, and I want to stay with you.'

'It feels so good to hear those words from you. No matter what happens, I will remember them always. But you know what we must do.' She kissed him then, letting the warmth of his love sink into her bones.

'This could not last for ever,' he whispered.

'Perhaps, in a way, it shall,' she whispered back. 'We are happy now. And we shall be happy again. I am sure of it. But you need to do this one thing, to make it all right.'

Chapter Seventeen

When Adrian arrived back at his rooms it was well past breakfast, and he made no attempt to disguise his entry from Hendricks. The man was at the desk in the small sitting room, giving disapprovingly sharp rattles to the paper as he read, as though he could pretend that he had not been checking the clock and waiting for milord to come back from his whore.

Let him wait, said the irritable voice in Adrian's head. *What right does he have to complain about your behaviour, if he has been using your absence to put horns on you?* Had it been just yesterday morning that he had convinced himself that the man was guiltless, and that David was clearly mistaken about Emily's behaviour?

He struggled to calm himself, as he had lying awake in his lover's arms. It did not matter what had happened, now that it was too late to change anything. The best he could hope for was to contain the damage. He could hardly blame Hendricks for loving the woman he wanted. And if she had true feelings in return, his attempting to slaughter Emily's lover might break her heart. And nothing he did now would make him any less a cuckold.

He stared in the direction of the rattling paper and said in his most bland voice, 'If you will give me a few moments to prepare myself, then I will be ready for the post and the paper.'

'Very good, my lord.'

As the valet helped him to change, he could hear the sniff of disapproval at the condition of his cravat, and the ease with which the man had noticed that it had been tied by hands other than Adrian's.

On any other day, he would have found it amusing. But today, a part of him wished that he could tell the man to take the razor and slice it up the back. After today, there was a chance that it was the only evidence he would have of the touch of *her* hands, anywhere in his life.

And his valet might as well follow the act by slitting his throat. He had lain there, after they had spoken of the future. And much as his mind had wanted to begin again, and to love her until he forgot what was to come, his body had found it impossible. He had done nothing but let her hold him. He had dozed as their last hours together ticked away, waiting to see the hazy glow of sunlight that was still allowed him.

And when he'd awakened enough to listen, he could tell by her breathing that she slept soundly, as though she had no fears. Perhaps her feelings had not been as she'd claimed. Faced with their inevitable parting, it had not caused so much as a bad dream for her. And when the sun was fully up, she'd woken, washed and dressed him, and sent him out of her life with a hearty breakfast and a kiss upon the cheek.

Halfway through his shave, Hendricks came into the room and went to the little table, bringing a cup of tea and lemon and forcing it into his hand.

Much as he wanted it, he said, 'Pour this out and bring me another. Just the tea. No sugar. No lemon.' Perhaps some day, when he felt himself starting to forget her. But not today.

'Very good, my lord.'

Hendricks returned shortly with the corrected cup, and drew up a chair and his little writing desk, and began reading the mail. And Adrian allowed the ordinariness of it soothe his mind, pretending that nothing had changed between them.

After dispensing with a tailor's bill and an invitation to a ball that Adrian had set aside as a possible peace offering to Emily, Hendricks said, 'The next is from your cousin Rupert.'

Adrian took a sip from his cup. 'Must we?'

'Hmm.' There was a pause as Hendricks scanned the letter. 'If you will trust my opinion, my lord? No. It is more of the same, really. He saw you yesterday?'

'At White's,' Adrian affirmed.

'He wishes to see you again.'

'How unfortunate for him.'

'There is the matter of your wife...'

'My response is the same as always,' Adrian snapped. 'Throw it on the fire.'

'Very good, my lord.'

And for the first time, Adrian wondered how much of his mail was read properly, and how much Hendricks had chosen to censor. For there was a chance that each letter he had received from Rupert had been full of warnings that his secretary had not seen fit to convey. 'Hendricks.'

'My lord?'

Adrian reached into the pocket in his coat, and held out the locket containing the miniature. 'Describe this to me.'

'It is Lady Folbroke, my Lord,' said the man, puzzled.

'But what does it look like?'

'It is done on ivory. In the painting, she is younger. Sixteen, perhaps. Her hair is longer and darker than it is now. Her face not so full.'

'And the quality of the work?'

'It does not do her justice, my lord.'

'I see.' And he had been displaying the ruined picture to the man for who knew how long, with no mention of it, with no clue that things were not as he thought they were.

'I mean to write to her, today.'

'Will you be needing my help, my lord?'

'No. This is something I must do for myself.' *Then I shall hope that you are not so far gone in love for her that you do not deliver the letter. For I know we are rivals for her affection, even if you do not admit it.*

There was a rattle as Hendricks opened the desk drawer and got out the little frame that Adrian some-times used to help him in his rare correspondence, with the notches to space the letters and the little bar on the paper so he could write a straight line. He arranged the pen and ink, explaining the location of each item as he placed them. Then he stood back to allow Adrian the seat.

'A few minutes' privacy, please, Mr Hendricks.' God knew, the composing of the thing would be hard enough without having to concern himself with other eyes than his catching sight of the letter.

'Very good, my lord.'

When he was sure that the valet and secretary had left him alone in the room, he put pen to ink, and hoped for the best.

Dear Emily,

Now he was lost as to what he must say next. He got the little miniature back out of his pocket, rubbed his finger across the face of it again and set it next to the letter. It did not matter what was truly there. For a little while longer, he must believe in what he wanted to see.

Almost without thinking, he picked it up and touched it again. It had been years since he'd seen Emily. And now that she was lost to him, he regretted not having looked at her more when he'd had the chance.

He dipped his pen again.

How are you faring in London?

No, that would not do. She would look at the line and think that if her welfare concerned him, he should have come and seen for himself long before now. Hendricks had said she'd thrown the last letter into the fire, just as he had the note from Rupert.

But he could not very well lead with a demand that she reveal the identity of her lover. Or a description of the events that had made his contacting her necessary. There had to be some preamble, some words that she would want to hear that would make her read more than a line or two.

And so he wrote the words that he knew she most deserved to hear.

I am sorry. Sorry for so many things that I hardly know where to start. But you have felt the sting of my neglect, and could give me a beginning, if I asked. Was it worse that I abandoned you? Or that I married you at all in the slipshod, neglectful way that I did, never asking your opinion in the matter, or taking the time to know your mind on the subject? I am sure that rumours of my disgraceful behaviour in London have reached you. Too many of those rumours are true. And I am sorry for the shame that they might have caused you.

And for burdening you with the responsibility of my property and all that it entails, I am equally sorry. If it gave you pleasure, then I am glad of it. But if it caused you pain or worry to take on the part of a man while receiving none of the privileges, then I am sorry for that as well.

He paused to wet his pen again. How could he tell her the rest?

> I wish to assure you that none of what has happened between us is any fault of yours. In many ways, you are a better wife than I deserved.

All perfectly true, if a trifle understated.

> The fault lies with me.

I am blind.
Say it, he commanded himself, as though he could order his hand to move and write the words. *Just say it. No dancing about.*

> There are certain impediments to our marriage.

No, that was not right. It sounded as if he had another wife.

> Problems.

And that was too small. She was well aware that there were problems, unless she was as blind as he.

> I am unable to be the husband that you deserve.

And that made him sound impotent. He cast another paper to the floor. He began again.

> I have been hiding from you the cause of our separation. I find that I am unable to explain the

difficulty, and my conscience can no longer bear the weight of the secret. Were I to come into your presence, it would be plain enough. And so, my dear, I think it is time that we talked. If you are as bothered by this prolonged separation as I am, then I would have you come to my rooms this evening to discuss it. And if you are not, then I will plead all the harder that you grant me an hour of your time. If you cast this on the fire, as you did the last missive, know that I will not relent until we have spoken.

I think I have guessed the reason for your recent visit, and there are things that must be settled between us before any more time passes. For my part, I wish to begin again and start fresh as though the last years that passed have never occurred.

If you do not, I can hardly blame you. If another has captured your affection, then I am glad for him and will regret my folly for waiting too long and losing the chance for happiness between us.

Either way, if you come to me tonight, you need have no fear of reproach. You will find me a humbled man, willing to take any course of action that puts your happiness ahead of my own. With my most heartfelt respect…

His pen hovered for a moment and added, 'and love', before signing his name. After the last week, it would be a lie to say that she had all his love. But she held the place closest to his heart.

And now, he began the other letter that he knew he must write. He scribbled the words hurriedly, not caring how they would look, just wishing to be done with it before he changed his mind, or said something he might regret. Then he blotted the ink, and fumbled for the wax and seal as he waited for it to cool. He addressed only one paper with a name and called for Hendricks, handing his secretary the two letters.

'One to my lover. If you do not know by now how to reach her, then wait for evening and send this back in the carriage I know she will send. And the other...' he moved the second letter carefully to the side '...to Emily.' He smiled. 'And careful not to confuse the two. That would be rather embarrassing.'

From the silence from the man, and his rather abrupt movement in reaching for the papers, Adrian could feel the disapproval crackling in the air.

'I know you think less of me because of my behaviour towards Emily, Hendricks.'

'I have no opinion on the matter, my lord.'

'Nonsense. If you weren't so damned polite, you'd have told me so to my face, long before now.'

There was another telling silence, rather than the quick denial of an honest man.

'If it is any consolation to you, there will be no more of this after today. I have chosen in a way that will do credit to my family and to myself.'

'Very well, my lord.' Hendricks was a good man. But he could not manage to sound pleased by this either, managing to say too much, in no words at all.

'But while I have much to be ashamed of, and much to apologise for, I cannot feel guilty for what has happened. Although I have tried to do so, I simply cannot. The woman I have been with has loved me. Truly, and for myself. Not the title, but the man and all his flaws. It is not something I have experienced before. It was a wonderful thing, Hendricks.'

'I would not know, sir.'

Adrian bit his tongue to hide his surprise. Was it possible that he had misunderstood the reason for the man's hesitance when speaking of Emily? Or perhaps it was that she did not return his feelings for her. If so, there was hope for him, though it might come at the expense of his friend.

But then, who was the source of the rumours about her?

And here was another unexpected gift from his lover. The sudden ability to feel sorry for someone other than himself. 'That is truly a pity, Hendricks. I hope, for your sake, that your circumstances change. Love, whether given or received, is transformative, in and of itself.'

And then he sat back in the desk, knowing that there was little for him to do but wait.

Chapter Eighteen

Emily sipped her morning chocolate, stretching luxuriously under the silk wrapper she wore. Lord, but she was stiff. And it made her blush to think of the reason for those sore muscles. Her darling Adrian had loved her quite enthusiastically.

And he had loved his wife as well. Her heart had ached afterwards almost as much as her body did now, to see him curled against her, broken by his betrayal of both the women he imagined were a part of his life. And she had wanted to reveal herself to him, to ease his suffering.

But a small part of her had cautioned her to stay silent. And as she thought about it, that bit had grown, reminding her that he was not the only one to suffer for his actions. Her misery had lasted for nearly the whole time she had known him. And his could last a day more. At least until his repentance bore fruit, and he made some kind of overture to the woman he had promised before God to cherish.

There was a knock at the door, and her maid informed her that Mr Hendricks was waiting in the sitting room with news for her. Emily gave a quick glance in the mirror to be sure that the robe she wore was decent enough to receive company, tightened the belt under her breasts and went out to greet her husband's secretary.

He held two sealed papers out to her and said, 'He has written to you. In both your guises. I was instructed to be sure not to confuse the letters, to take the first one immediately to his wife, and that if I did not know the direction to you here, to send this with the coach that would come for him in the evening.'

'I see.' So whatever he had to say, he meant to speak first to his wife on the matter. Emily weighed the two pieces of paper in her hand, trying to guess the contents without opening them, and nodded absently to Hendricks, directing him to await her replies.

Did it really matter which she opened first? For if she had read the situation correctly, they would be two sides of the coin. She must trust, now that she had met the man, that the pair of them were not full of lies.

She cracked the seal on the one that bore no name, and read.

My love.

It is with difficulty that I pen these words to you. More than the usual difficulty, of course.

So he had taken the time to joke with her? The news must be bad, indeed.

> But it seems some things are better written, for they prevent me from avoiding what could be an unpleasant truth.

In this, she was very much in sympathy.

> I have taken your suggestion, and written to Emily, in hopes of resolving the difficulties in our marriage. After last night, I proved to both of us that I cannot leave the spectre of her between us any longer. And I know that you will understand when I say I have no desire to hurt you, any more than I did my poor wife.

Obviously. Her eyes rushed down the uneven lines on the page.

> And know also that I would not have had the nerve to face this, had it not been for the time spent in your arms. It has brought about a change in me. A change for the better.

She smiled, thinking how nice it was that he would say so.

> This evening, should my wife desire it, I will return home to face what future there is for me, and you will see me no more. I beg you, my darling, understand that I would not leave you were it my

choice. For this time we have spent together has been some of the happiest of my life. The past days with you have been closer to perfection than any man deserves. And thus, I fear, they cannot last.

Your words of love were not unwelcome. And though I wish I could say otherwise, I hold honour too dear to reciprocate them. My first obligation must be to the woman I married, and I can no longer fulfil it from a distance, any more than your husband can for you.

Emily had his duty. Which was all well and good. But love would be better.

If my wife rejects me, which I fear is quite possible, then I will write to you immediately and you will know that my heart has no claim on it. It is yours to command, should you still wish it. Half of it is already yours, and always will be.

But whether we be together or parted, Emily has the other half. And the better portion, for it was the one I gave first.

She stopped reading for a moment, and looked at the other letter, wondering if it was half as sweet. Then she returned to the one in her hand.

If I had known you three years ago, I like to think that things might have been different and that I would be at your side today. But if you have the love for me that you claim to, I pray you, wish me well in this most difficult decision and let me go. I must try to make my Emily happy, just as I wish you all the happiness in the world.

For ever yours, Adrian.

Without thinking, she clutched the paper to her lips and kissed it. Then she tore the seal on the next letter, and read what he had to say to his wife.

It was cautious. Polite. And shorter. And when she got to the line about his being humbled, she almost laughed aloud. Even in humbleness, he was more proud than any two other men.

But his willingness to put her pleasure before his own? She thought of how he had treated her when he took her to bed. He had proven that he could do that so often that it made her blush to think about it.

She kissed the second letter as well. Fondly at first. And then touching her tongue quickly to the paper and thinking of how it would be, tonight, when she came to him in his own bed. A marriage bed. Just as it ought to have been between them all along.

Was this not the best of both worlds? She was his lover, and had half his heart for the asking. And she was his wife as well, and commanded his honour and loyalty, along with the rest of his love. He would be her faithful servant, if she wished to take him back. And though he came to her with head bowed, she would make sure that he lost nothing by it. They would both gain by his homecoming.

Once they got past the surprise he would get on learning her identity.

Emily smiled to herself and dismissed it. Surely that would be as nothing. It would set his mind to rest to realise that the woman he loved and the woman he had married were one and the same.

From his place in front of her, Hendricks cleared his throat, reminding her that she was not alone. 'Well?'

She smiled up at him. 'He has chosen me. *Me*. Emily.'

The man at her side looked confused, as though he did not see a distinction. 'Was there ever any doubt?'

'Surprisingly, there was. And now I must go to him, and explain the meaning of his choice, as gently as possible.'

'I suppose you will expect me to come along in this, to support you when it goes wrong.' Hendricks was glaring at her. His tone was sharp, as though he had any right to question her activities.

'I do not expect you to make the explanation for me, if that is what you fear,' she said back, equally annoyed. 'It is my husband who leaves you to write his messages for him, not I.'

'While you have never made me write them, you have had no qualms in making me carry them,' he reminded her. 'You have forced me to lie to a man who is not just my employer, but an old friend.'

'As he forced you to lie to me,' she said.

'But he did it in an effort to protect you,' Hendricks answered. 'Can you say the same?'

'What makes you think you can question me on my

marriage? After all this time, neither of you has cared to inform me of the truth. If I choose to keep a secret for a matter of days, you have no right to scold me.'

'I do not do it to scold,' he said, more softly, 'but because I know Folbroke and his pride. He will think you did what you did to amuse yourself with his ignorance.'

'And now, after all this time, I do not know if I care,' she admitted. 'If what I have done annoys him? Then it will pay him back for the hurt I suffered, all the time he has been away. When he did not know me, and I told him the truth of our marriage, he did not recognise that, any more than he did me. He thought my husband's treatment of me was unfair. And he had admitted the same of his treatment to his wife.'

'Then you must realise that he has suffered as well,' Hendricks said.

She spread her arms wide, to encompass the problem. 'And tonight, he will apologise for it. And I will apologize for tricking him. And then the matter will be settled.'

Hendricks laughed. 'You really think it will be that easy. And have you thought what you will do if he does not forgive you? He might well cast you off for this. And if he does, he will be in far worse shape than you found him in.'

'It will not come to that,' she insisted, but suddenly felt a doubt.

'If it does, he will not last long. You will have taken his hope from him. It might be more merciful of you to leave him with that than to bring him a truth that comes too late.'

What good would it do her to leave him his fantasy, and destroy any hope she had that they would ever be together? And what would become of her, if she could not have him?

Then she remembered Adrian's suspicions about his secretary's interest in the unobtainable Emily. And she said the words that she was sure both dreaded, but that needed to be spoken. For if there was any truth in what her husband took as a fact, than she must settle it now, once and for all. 'Mr Hendricks, if there is something else you have to say on your hopes for my future, then you had best say it, and clear the air between us. But before you do, know that I decided on the matter from the first moment I laid eyes on Adrian Longesley, many years ago and long before I met you. Nothing said by another is likely to change me on the subject at this late date.'

She waited in dread that Hendricks might speak what he was really thinking and thus ruin their friendship and any chance of his continued employment. There was a pause that was longer than simple circumspection. And then, he said nothing more than a curt, 'I understand that, my lady. And I have nothing to say.' And for a moment, she could see that he smouldered with frustration and a range of other emotions inappropriate to his station. Then they submerged beneath the surface again, leaving him the placid and efficient secretary she had grown to depend on. 'I will accompany you this evening to assure

Lord Folbroke that there is no hidden motivation to your actions, and that all was done in his best interest. But I suspect that although he may say he loves you both, it might not extend to an easy forgiveness to all of us who have had a part in this attempt at reconciliation.'

As the afternoon changed to evening, Adrian paced the floor of his sitting room, wondering if he had done the right thing. After a few false moves, he had learned to correct his course to avoid the pianoforte that still blocked the corner. And he wondered—would he ever have to explain the thing? Or would Emily take it as a given that it had come with the rooms? Perhaps she would expect him to show some interest in playing it, just as its giver had done.

If she did, he would admit his ignorance, but would submit meekly to lessons, if they were necessary to keep the peace. And if, each time he touched the keys, he thought of someone else?

It would be better if he did not think of the thing at all, and suggest they remove to Derbyshire. It would give them a chance to discuss their differences in private, and he would be far from temptation. And if necessary, it would disguise the length of Emily's confinement.

He squeezed his eyes tightly shut, realising that it made no difference. His progress across the room was unaffected, and it did nothing to shut out the pictures in his mind of his wife growing big with another man's child. One did not need eyes to see one's thoughts.

But he had told himself for over a year that this was

likely to happen, and that it would not bother him. Now he must survive the future he'd created with as much grace as he could manage. Tonight could not be about recriminations. He had promised something quite different in his letter.

And had that been the correct course of action? Perhaps it would have been better to go to her, rather than expecting her to come to him? It would have shown more respect.

And that would have left him fumbling his way through Eston's town house, demonstrating the worst of his condition before he had a chance to speak to her. Or, worse yet, he'd have discovered she was at her rooms.

'Hendricks?'

'He has not yet returned, my lord,' said the footman who had come into the room to bring his afternoon tea.

Now Adrian imagined his secretary and his wife in the process of a tearful parting, spending a languid afternoon alone in each other's arms.

He sat and took a sip of tea, scalding his tongue and focusing on the real pain instead of the imagined one. He must not doubt his choices, now that they had been made. Here, in his own home, he could show to best advantage that he was not the helpless invalid she might fear him to be. He had told his man to take care with his dressing, that everything about him must be just so, clean and unrumpled. And he had not taken so much as a drop of wine with his noon meal, that there would be no evidence of excess in his diet. He would hold himself with a posture worthy of a dress parade, so that, in the first glance she had of him after so much time, she would think him strong, capable and worthy.

Yet he knew them to be superficial changes that might not be enough. Perhaps it would be better if he were not alone for this. He was blind. And he had not told her. There was no way to excuse that.

He called out to the footman, 'Parker, I wish to see Mr David Eston. Send someone to his rooms and request his presence, tonight, a little before seven. Explain to him that his sister will be visiting me. And that we may require his assistance in a delicate matter.' Her brother could act as a buffer between them and escort Emily home, should the worst occur and she rejected him.

But if she was truly in a delicate condition, it was unfair of him to expect her to weather this alone.

Chapter Nineteen

That night, Emily twisted nervously upon the hand-kerchief in her hands as they came into her husband's lodgings. Hendricks glanced at her and then at the footman, waving aside an announcement of their entrance. Then he threw himself down on a bench by the front door as though he suspected the need for a hasty retreat and gestured towards the sitting-room door. 'He will be there, waiting for you,' he said in a surly voice. 'I am staying here. Call if you need me.' He glared up at the footman, as though daring the man to find anything odd about the situation and said, 'Parker, bring me a brandy. A large one.' And then he stared at the opposite wall as though he had arrived alone and unwelcome in the home of strangers.

Emily walked down the hall and away from him, hesi-tating on the threshold of the room where she knew her husband waited.

But the pause had been without purpose, for she could not have turned and left unnoticed. Adrian's head lifted eagerly at the faint scuffling of her slippers. 'Emily?' He listened for the clock. 'You are early.' He stood at her approach and her heart nearly stopped at the look on his face and the way he reached out to the doorway, welcoming her through it. He was wearing a coat of midnight-blue wool that lay smooth over his broad shoulders. Black trousers covered his well-shaped legs without a wrinkle. His cravat was a Mathematical and starched to an almost painful formality, and his boots gleamed in the candlelight as though his valet had made it a life's mission to show her the reflection of her entrance back into her husband's life.

It was a stark contrast to the casual handsomeness that he normally showed her. He had wished to look his best when they finally met.

And then he seemed to lift his face and scent the air. There was a growing look of alarm in his blank eyes. He had recognised her even before she spoke.

'Adrian?' she said softly.

His hand dropped and his smile faltered, becoming a frown. 'I am sorry. I was not expecting...'

'Perhaps you were.'

They both paused then, trying to decide who should speak next. She closed the distance between them, coming behind his desk to lay her hands on his face in reassurance. He closed his fingers over hers and felt the ring she had taken from her jewellery case for the occasion.

'Your wedding ring,' he said.

'It belonged to your mother,' she reminded him. 'I have not been wearing it for some time. It is quite heavy. And I found the continual reminder...difficult.' Then she brushed his fingers over her own features so there could be no doubt that he knew her for who she was. 'There is something I must explain to you.'

'I expect there is.' His voice was as crisp and tight as his cravat.

'Our first meeting was not by chance. I sought you out.'

'I know that,' he said. 'But I did not know that you had found me.' He pulled his hand from her grasp and away from her face.

'Mr Hendricks warned me that I would not like what I found.'

'Hendricks.' Adrian gave her a cool smile. 'Why am I not surprised that he was involved in this?'

'But I insisted he take me to you. I did not know how horrible the place was, and when you rescued me...'

'Lucky for you that I did, my lady,' he said. 'To go there demonstrated no care for your virtue or your safety.'

It had not bothered him so much when he had thought her another man's wife. But perhaps she deserved his scorn. 'I was wrong. I know that now, and will not make the same mistake again. But you saved me from my own foolishness. And you were so heroic. And when you kissed me? It was just as I'd always imagined it could be.'

He pulled her close to him suddenly, and the contact was more frightening than comforting. 'And now you will tell me that you have spent our time apart, dreaming of the taste of my lips. Please spare me the poetry, for there is much more to this story, I am sure.'

She turned her head away from his sightless stare. For the first time since she'd found him, it was unsettling her. 'I wanted to be with you. But there was so much wrong.'

'Finally. We come to the meat of it,' he said.

'What if you laughed at me? What if you rejected me, once you knew?'

He pushed her away from him, and turned away from her to face the fire. 'And in an unguarded moment, I told you that such a rejection was unlikely. That I suspected already, and would forgive you anything. Why did you not tell me the truth then?'

She struggled to remember what he had said that might have been a cue to a revelation, and could think of not one thing that mattered more than any other. 'I did not tell you because I did not want what we were doing to end. It had not yet been as it was last night.'

'But now that I have planted my seed in you, you have nothing to fear. You know there is no chance I will cast you off, now that you might carry my heir.'

'Adrian,' she said, disappointed, 'that is not what I meant at all.'

'Then perhaps you should explain again. For I fail to see any other logical explanation for your behaviour.'

There was a commotion from the hall. The sound of Hendricks's voice raised in protest, and the curt dismissal of someone who had no intention of listening to him. Parker's voice was raised as well, so that he could be heard over the din and making his usual offers of assistance and announcement.

'Emily.' Her brother burst into the room, staring at the two of them together. 'It is about time that you have come to your senses. When I heard that you were invited here tonight, I was afraid I would have to drag you to the meeting. Or do you think that this is the result of your plans to sort your affairs?'

'David. What are you doing here?'

Adrian said, more to the fireplace than to them, 'I invited him because I feared that the shock of discovering my condition might unsettle your delicate nerves.'

'Your condition?' David strode across the room to her husband and seized him by the shoulder, passing a hand in front of his face. 'Adrian, what is this I hear about you from Anneslea? It is a joke, is it not, for I saw you just last week.'

'But I did not see you,' Adrian responded, laughing bitterly, and slapped his hand away. 'I have enough sight left to know that you are waggling your fingers in front of my eyes, trying to catch me in a trick. I can see the shadow of them. But that is all. Now stop it, or I will find sight enough to thrash you for the impudence of it.'

'And you let me stand here yammering at you the other day and said nothing about a problem. You let me think you were drunk. Or were you drunk? I no longer know what to believe out of you.' She could see the anger and confusion clouding David's face, and held up a warning hand, hoping that he would not muddy the situation any more than it already was.

'You can safely believe that I did not tell you, because it was none of your damned business. Any of it,' her husband snapped. Then he pushed David away and walked back to her, grabbing her by the arm and pulling her to his side. A hand came up to her face, and his head cocked to the side as he traced the lines of her, as though trying to replace this image with the one he held in his mind. His other hand released her, reaching for the miniature, as though there were some way left to compare the two.

'Then you shouldn't have invited me into the middle of things tonight,' David shouted at the back of his head. 'And you.' Her brother stared at her, almost shaking with rage. 'It was him, all along, wasn't it? I do not know which is worse—that you do not admit to the world that you are together again, or that you could not at least admit it to me.'

Adrian smiled at her. And his expression was so cold and heartless that she was glad he could not see her fear. 'Oh, I think there is much more that needs to be confessed, if you wish to know the whole of the story, isn't there, Emily?'

'Certainly not.' Surely he did not expect her to tell her own brother the most intimate details of the last few days.

'You could at least assure David that he was right in his assumptions about your entertaining another gentleman under our very noses.'

'I beg your pardon?' Where had he gotten such ideas?

Adrian looked at her brother. 'Your little sister has led me a merry dance, David. She tricked me into thinking she was another woman, rather than admitting from the first that she was my wife. She would not even give me a name, because she said I would know her in an instant, should she give me the smallest clue to her identity.' He laughed. 'And I have been dangling after her for days like a lovesick idiot, racked with guilt at my betrayal of my wife and the depths of feeling I had developed for this supposed stranger.'

David was staring at her, his anger stifled by bafflement. 'Why would you do such a foolish thing, Emily? Would not the truth have been simpler?'

'Oh, I think the answer is obvious,' Adrian announced. 'She came to London to trick me into bed, hoping that she could hide the evidence of her infidelity. And when she realised that I could not see, she found it good sport to trick me with lies. I hope that you have gotten sufficient amusement from our time together. For I certainly have.'

She gasped in fury at the thought that he might refer to the things they had done together, even in such an oblique way. 'Of course, Adrian. Because why would I not find it amusing that my husband had been so long away from me that he did not even know me? Or to have evidence of your frequent infidelity thrust in my face?'

'My infidelity?' he shouted back. 'At least you did not have to drink endless toasts to celebrate the results of it, as I did for you at White's.'

'I have no idea what you are talking about,' she said, angry, but still confused.

'When, exactly, am I to expect the heir you seem to have got for me? Or is the date of delivery to be as much of a surprise as the parentage?'

'I say…' David sputtered, ready, once again, to come to her defence. 'Emily, are you…?'

'Oh, hush,' she said, glaring at him. 'If you have nothing constructive to add, then please refrain from speaking.' She turned to Adrian and said, 'I did not tell you the truth because it was apparent, almost from the first day we married, that you wished no part of me.'

'If my treatment bothered you, then you could have spared yourself the trip to London and written me on the matter. If you had explained your dissatisfaction, we might have discussed the matter like adults.'

She could feel him growing distant again, as though it were possible at this late date to go back to the way they had been. 'If you had bothered to answer my letters at all. Or told me the whole truth when you did. I had to come to London to see you, to learn about the loss of your sight.'

'And when you did, you thought it would be easy to trick a blind fool into thinking he'd got you with child so that you would not have to explain yourself.'

'I have done nothing that needs an explanation. But if you wish to think of yourself as a fool,' she said, 'then far be it from me to change your mind. It is clear enough to me that you are little hampered by your condition, when you want something. It is only when you do not get your way that you insist on reminding people of it. If I turned to childish subterfuge, it was in response to my adversary.'

'I am your adversary now, am I?' He smiled again, as though satisfied that he understood the situation at last. 'On second thought, it is well that you came to see me, so that I could know the way of things. It seems that my idealised view of my little country wife was quite naïve. You run the estate because I allow it, and now you have arranged for my successor. And in all the recent foolishness, I have forgotten how well the arrangement suits me. I will return to my diversions, and you may return to Derbyshire with your bastard, secure in the knowledge that I will offer no objections.' He turned to go into his bedroom and her brother made to go after him.

She placed a hand on David's arm and pushed him firmly out of the way. 'I am dismissed again, am I? And I suppose I should not be the least bit surprised by it. It is just as I suspected, from the first. Once you knew who I was, you would want nothing to do with me.'

He turned back to her. 'I do not want anything to do with a woman who would use my blindness to her own advantage against me.'

'To my advantage?' She laughed. 'And what advantage did I gain that I was not entitled to? In exchange for having you treat me as one might normally treat a wife, I have made every attempt to improve your character. I dare say the man I found was a drunken, suicidal wreck, too steeped in self-pity to be worthy of his estate, his title or the woman he'd married. And now, after the fine promises you made in the last day, you plan a return to that state. By all means, if it pleases you, make yourself as miserable as you do your wife and friends.'

His blank eyes glittered; for a moment, he looked as disappointed by the idea as she was. But then he regained control and stared through her, speaking as though he did not know or care if she was still in the room. 'This interview is at an end. I find further communication between us to be both unnecessary and unwelcome. If it is absolutely required, we will communicate through an intermediary.' He turned to walk back into his room. Then he turned back suddenly and said, 'And for the love of God, woman, choose someone other than Hendricks to carry your messages. Allow me that, at least.' Then he turned again and disappeared behind the slammed door.

Emily reached for her brother's arm before the trembling began, for the outpouring of emotion had made her almost physically weak. 'Take me home, David. I wish to go home.'

She did not have the heart to tell him that his obvious rage at her husband was totally lost on the man, who had not seen the dark scowls he was receiving from his own friend. He was helping her through the front door now, to his carriage.

And for a moment she thought she heard the sound she longed for. A call from the open door behind her, the sound of contrite footsteps hurrying down the tiles of the entry hall. A sign that her husband wanted her, now that he knew who she was.

But there was nothing. Only Hendricks, standing framed in the open doorway.

She turned away from him, far too confused to seek his comfort. Instead, she leaned upon her brother's arm with her whole weight, letting him lead her the rest of the way to her seat. When they were safely inside the carriage, she thought about allowing herself the luxury of tears. But they would only reveal what she suspected her brother already knew: how deeply Adrian's latest rejection had hurt her.

David was staring out of the back window in the direction of Adrian's flat, as though he could not quite believe how suddenly and totally wrong the evening had been. Then, he turned to her, accusing her with his eyes. 'You could at least have told me about the child.'

'There is no child,' she snapped.

'Then why did he think there was?'

'Possibly because my own brother came to warn him about my affair.' She hoped he did not expect some sort of absolution for all the trouble his meddling had caused her.

'I am sorry. I did not know.'

She said, 'You could not be expected to. The circumstances were…unusual. But in future, when I request you not to intervene, I would appreciate your co-operation.' Then she remembered the comment about his afternoon at his club. 'And I think it was Rupert who misled him about my supposed pregnancy. You only added fuel to the fire.'

Her brother fell silent for a time, and then said, 'Perhaps, once he has had time to think, he will relent and come to you.'

'Or perhaps not. He is a very proud man. And I have hurt him.'

'He is afraid of exposure.'

'He is no coward,' she argued.

'Of course not,' her brother said in a voice dripping with sarcasm. 'He merely hid a problem from us, for our own good. He feared the family would remove the title from him.' And then he added more thoughtfully, 'There is a chance we could do it, you know. He has been behaving little better than a madman, shirking his responsibilities, risking life and limb. Perhaps we could arrange an annulment, if this is a family condition. If you had been together, then the children—'

'No,' she snapped back. 'There is nothing wrong with his mind. It is only his eyes.' She glared at her brother, daring him to oppose her. 'You were quick enough to marry me off to him when he was your friend. And still content when he left me. You cannot just grab me back, three years down the road, because you fear that he is likely to leave me childless and lose the entail.'

'It is not that at all, Emily.' David groaned in frustration. 'Why must everyone expect the worst from me? Can you truly be happy with him, in his condition? He will be helpless, and you will need to care for him, just as you would a child.'

'You know nothing of him, and what he can do,' she said hotly. 'He is quite capable, when he has a mind to be. As sharp as he ever was. And if he needs my help?'

She lifted her chin. 'I have been waiting for the chance to be his helpmeet for some time. And if there is to be a baby, there can be no question of it being anyone's but his.'

Her brother raised his hands in front of him, in a gesture of helplessness, as though afraid to ask for further explanation. 'I swear, it all grows more confusing, the longer you explain it to me.'

'It is very simple. All that I have done, I've done out of love for Adrian. And I think, given the time, he will realise that he feels the same for me.'

David looked at her doubtfully. 'Very well. If a reconciliation with him is what you wish, then I hope you succeed in it. But after today's interview, it appears that Adrian is just as stubborn as he ever was at avoiding his marriage to you.'

And remembering what she had told herself on coming to London, she should be satisfied with the results of the visit. She had been with him, in the way a wife should be with a husband. She had assured herself that he was indeed alive, and Rupert had been assured of his well-being. She had ascertained the reason for his absence. If he continued to remain apart from her, she would at least know why. And in the end she had managed to speak clearly to him and to make him well aware of her displeasure at the separation.

She had succeeded in all the things she'd set out to do.

And done the one thing she had never meant to. She had fallen truly in love with her husband.

Chapter Twenty

When his guests had left him, Adrian stormed back to his sitting room, still furious with the way he had been tricked. Emily had known him from the first moment. And had taunted him with the knowledge the whole time they had been together. How she must have laughed, to hold that from him, just out of reach.

The servants had known as well, for they had known her when she'd brought him home from the tavern. And Hendricks had been complicit in the elaborate scheme, for she could not have managed it without his help. Everyone surrounding him had kept mum on the truth, smirking as he mooned over his own wife, pitying him for the poor blind fool he was.

If they had the time to laugh, then perhaps they did not have enough to occupy their time. He swept a hand across his desk in the corner, sending pen, inkwell and writing frame all to the floor in a heap. He pulled down the books on the shelves as well, useless things that they were now that he could not see them. He upended the piano stool, and wishing he had discovered enough about the instrument to destroy the thing so that it would never trouble him with memories again. He slammed the lid down over the keys, and his fingers touched the decanter of brandy that had been set on top of it. To a man who did not play, such a thing was little better than a makeshift table.

His fingers closed around the neck of the bottle and he imagined the sound of shattering crystal, and the sight of the brandy, running in fine rivulets down the wall, or dripping amongst the piano strings, and the pungent scent of the spilled liquor…

Then he stopped. It would be better to drink the stuff than to waste a chance at oblivion. No need for a glass…

His arm froze with the bottle halfway to his mouth, and he held it there. How much of the last year had he spent just that way? Blundering about, breaking things and drinking. Time drifting by, and him neither knowing nor caring how it passed. How long had it been since he had given up even trying to care?

His Emily had been waiting at home for him, doing her best. She had said as much, hadn't she, when she'd told him about her marriage? How she worried that it had been her fault he'd left. And how frightened she had been at first that he would reject her again. She had been sure that if he ever really knew her, it would be all over between them. He had made it his mission to prove otherwise.

In the end, she had been right. The moment he had learned her identity, he'd sent her away.

She had been quite accepting of his truth when she had learnt it. He had assured her that there was nothing on earth his wife could do to lose his trust, for the fault of their parting had been his, and his alone.

Still holding the brandy, he stooped to the floor, fumbling to pick up the books around his feet. How much damage had he done in his rush to destroy what he could not appreciate? The wreckage around him was the result of another selfish act on his part. Just one of many in the last few years.

But when had he ever learned to be otherwise? He thought of how angry he had been with his father's foolish disregard for the future of the family. And how angry his father had been, when talking of Grandfather. All of them angry at fate for the hand that they had been dealt.

But while Emily might be cross with him for his treatment of her, she worked to change the things that made her unhappy and made the best of the rest.

She accepted him.

He took a deep breath and walked through the debris to the door, opening it suddenly on the shadow waiting in the hall.

'Hendricks.'

'Yes, milord.' It was not the usual calm tone of his old friend, but the clipped words of a man simmering with rage.

Adrian cleared his throat, wishing he could call back

any of the last fifteen minutes. 'It seems I have had an embarrassing display of temper.'

'I can see that.'

'It will not happen again.'

'Not to me, at least. I am giving my notice.'

For a moment, he felt the same as he had when his eyes started to fail him. As though everything he'd taken for granted had slipped away. 'You can't be serious.'

'I am always serious, sir. You comment often on my lack of humour.'

'It was never an issue, when we met,' Adrian reminded him. 'On the Peninsula, you were quite good company.'

'And you never used to be such a damned fool.' The blow seemed to come from nowhere as Hendricks kicked the brandy bottle from his hand. It hit the floor with a thump, and Adrian could hear the glug of the liquid spilling from it, and the smell of it soaking into the rug.

'Perhaps not.' Adrian stood, straightening to full height and taking a step forwards, knowing that whether he saw it or not, he still towered over his friend. It would not be wise to let him think he could strike twice. 'But then I did not have to worry about you lying to me to cement your position with my wife. You have known of this charade from the beginning, haven't you?'

'Of course. Because I am not blind.' Hendricks had added the last to goad him, he was sure.

'I can think of only one reason that you would go along with such nonsense. Rupert told me, yesterday, that Emily was with child.'

Hendricks gave a hiss of surprise, and stifled an oath.

'And I assume that the child is yours, and that you rushed her to London so that she might lie with me as well and there would be some assumption of legitimacy.' Adrian laughed. 'Why you would think such a thing might work, I have no idea. I do not need my eyesight to count to nine.'

Hendricks swore aloud now, as Adrian had not heard him do since their days in the army. 'You really are an idiot, Folbroke. And it amazes me that I had not noticed it before now. Do you wish to hear how I found your wife, when I went to her today?'

'The truth from you would be a welcome change,' Adrian snapped back.

'Very well, then. When I saw her this morning, she was nothing like that silly picture you carry of her. The miniature that you have worn to the bone with your fondling is of a rather plain, ordinary young girl. But the woman I saw today was fresh from bed, and wearing nothing but a blue silk wrapper. She had tied it tight under her breasts in a way that left little to the imagination. And as she sat, the skirt slipped open and I could see her ankles, and the slope of her bare calf.'

Adrian's hand clenched, wishing that he had the bottle again so that he could strike out at the voice and shut the man's mouth for good.

'She took the letters you sent her, and read both of them in quick succession. She sighed over them. She kissed them. She all but made love to the paper while I stood there like an idiot, admiring her body and wishing that just once she might give me an instruction that did not involve running back to you. But nothing has changed. In regards to men other than the Earl of Folbroke, she is every bit as blind as you are to her.'

'So you know nothing about this supposed child?'

There was a long pause, as though the next words were difficult. 'She has been faithful to you. From the moment you married. I would stake my life on it. There is no way she can be pregnant.'

'But at White's, Rupert said—'

Hendricks cut him off. 'If you had used the brains you used to have, you would consider the source of the rumour, and remember that your cousin is an even bigger fool than you.'

To the trained ear of someone who had no choice but to listen, there was as much emotion in the last speech as there had been in the first. Regret, frustration and jealousy of a husband so unworthy of the devotion he had received from his beautiful wife.

Adrian knew the feelings, for he had felt them himself when he'd thought of Emily.

'You are right,' Adrian said at last. 'If there is any truth at all, or any explanation that can be made, I should have asked her for it, rather than trusting the man who wants nothing more than to ensure that I do not have a child. And I think I understand your reasons for leaving me as well.' For how awkward would it be if Adrian apologised to his wife and they all went back to Derbyshire together. The two of them, living side by side in the same house, both loving the same woman? And all the worse for Hendricks, forced to witness their happiness, and to know that though Adrian was his equal in ability and his inferior in temperament, he had the superior rank, and the unwavering love of his countess.

He put the thoughts of Emily aside for the moment and said, 'You will have letters of reference, of course. And anything you might need.'

'I have already written them.'

Adrian laughed. 'I expected no less from you. You are damned efficient, when you set about to do something.' He stepped over the bottle on the floor and gripped the man by the hand. 'I trust that I was effusive in my praise of you. And generous in my severance?'

'Of course, my lord.'

'I expected nothing less of me. You have been invaluable as an aide. And you shall always be welcome in my house, as a guest, should you ever wish to return there.'

'I do not think I will be back for some time,' Hendricks said. 'If things go as I expect, you will be too busy for company, at least until after the new year.'

'Next year, then. The fishing is good in the run at Folbroke. You still fancy trout, do you not?'

'I do indeed, my lord.'

'Then you must be sure that the money I give to you in parting is enough so that you might live comfortably on it for twelve months and then visit me as a man of leisure before taking another post. I will not take no for an answer.'

'Of course, my lord.' It would have felt deuced odd to touch the man's face, after all these years. But suddenly, as though there had been a change between them, it was hard to read any truth in Hendricks's words. Adrian had heard the worry and frustration plain in the man's voice for so long that the sudden absence of it was like a void in the room. It had been foolish of him to think that there could ever be mockery or cruel deception. 'Hendricks, I am sorry. I understand that I have not been an easy master...'

'Lord Folbroke. There is no need—'

He held up a hand to forestall the man's excuses. 'It is true. But there will be no more nonsense after today. If you mean to leave me in the hands of my good wife, I will be an amiable man and not trouble her unnecessarily.'

'Very good, my lord.' There was blessed relief in the man's voice, as though he had given him compensation beyond money in that one little plan.

'Of course, I shall have to square things away again, after the mess I've just made of this interview.' He dropped out the statement in the most offhand way possible, as though the entire staff had not heard the argument that had just ensued. 'Eston has taken her back to his town house, I assume?'

'I believe so, sir. I could send for her, if you wish.'

'No, that is quite all right. I will go to her.'

'I will have the carriage brought round.'

'No.' An idea had suddenly occurred to him. 'It is less than a mile from here. And the night is clear, is it not?'

'Yes, my lord.'

'Then I shall walk.'

'I will have a footman accompany you.'

Adrian stood and reached out to grip his old friend's arm. 'If you mean to leave me to my own devices, then I will have to learn to do without you.' Although damned if he knew how. 'The streets are not crowded. And I remember the way. I will go alone.'

'Very good, sir.' There was only a trace of doubt in Hendricks's voice, which Adrian took to mean that he was not suggesting something beyond the realm of possibility. It was something he had never tried, of course. But his sight was unlikely to get any better. It was high time he learned to navigate the city. They walked together into the front hall, and instead of Parker coming to aid him, he felt the familiar hands of Hendricks helping him into his topcoat and handing him his hat and gloves. Then the door opened, and he sent Adrian on his way with a pat on the back.

And almost as an afterthought, there came from behind him a soft, 'Take care of her, Adrian.'

'I mean to, John.' Then he walked down the steps to the pavement and set out into what might as well have been a wilderness, for all he knew of it.

Chapter Twenty-One

Four steps down, to the street. He felt the edge of the kerb with his cane and stepped a little back from it. And now, a left. It would be two roads down in this direction, he remembered, before turning onto the busier street ahead. He listened closely as he set out, to gauge his surroundings. It was more difficult in darkness than it might have been in the light, for he could not use the rays of the sun to set a direction.

But for this first trip, it was better to be out when the way was not so crowded. He heard a single walker on the other side of the street from him, and remembered that he would have to be cautious of footpads and cutpurses. Though the areas he travelled were good ones, not all that ventured out after dark could be trusted.

He tapped ahead of him with his stick, to make sure there were no obstacles, and set out at a pace that was slower than normal, but still little different from a stroll. He almost stumbled, as the pavement gave way in another kerb. But then he caught himself and stood, looking both ways for changes in the shadows that obscured his sight, and listening for the sound of horses' hooves and the rattle of carts or carriages.

When he was sure there was nothing, he made sure his course was straight, stepped forwards, and made an uneventful crossing, gaining the opposite side. He proceeded for a little while longer in the same fashion, before everything began to go wrong.

He could hear the increase of traffic around him as the way became busier. While most passers-by gave him a safe space to walk in, he was occasionally jostled and forced to adjust his pace to those around him. The changes in speed made it harder to keep a straight course, and the corner seemed to come much sooner than he expected. Had he passed two or three streets?

Suddenly, he felt a hand, light as a moth's touch, on the pocket that held his purse.

He caught the tiny wrist easily in the fingers of his left hand. 'Here, you. What are you about?'

'Please, sir. I didn't mean nothing.' A child. A girl? No. A boy. He was sure of it; though the wrist he held was bony, it did not feel delicate, and the sleeve that it jutted from was rough wool.

'You just choose to walk with your hand in my pocket, then? No more of this nonsense, boy. You meant to have my purse. And now the Runners shall have you.'

'Please, sir…' there was the loud, wet sniff of a child

who was near tears and with a perpetual cold '…I didn't mean any harm. And I was hungry.'

'And I am blind, not stupid. And certainly not as insensate as you expected. I am much harder to sneak up upon, because I pay better attention to small things such as you.' He gave a frustrated sigh to persuade the boy that he was serious in his intent, but not without sympathy. Then he said, 'If you want to avoid the law, then you had best prove your worth. I am walking to St James's Square. Do you know the way?'

'Yes, sir. Of course.'

'Then take my hand and lead me the rest of the distance. Keep a sharp eye out and steer me clear of any pickpockets. And I will know if you lead me wrong, so do not try it, or it will be off to the Runners with you.' Then he pretended to soften. 'But if you lead me right, there will be a shilling for you, and a nice dinner.' And at the sound of another sniff, he added, 'And a clean handkerchief.'

'Yes, sir.'

He felt a small hand creep into his, and a tug, as the boy turned him, and set off at a brisk pace in the other direction. After a while, he could tell that the boy was honest, for the sounds around him and the echoes off the buildings of the square changed to something more like he had expected.

It annoyed him that, in his first outing, he had proved himself unable to find a house he had visited hundreds of times. Perhaps that meant that he was as helpless as he feared, a useless invalid that would only be a burden to his wife.

Or perhaps it proved that he would manage as best he could, under the circumstances. In any case, it had been better than hiding in his bedroom. Even having accepted aid, he felt an unaccustomed sense of power.

The boy read off the numbers to him as they passed, and then led him up to the door he specified. 'Here we are, sir.' The boy was hesitating as though afraid to lift the knocker.

For a moment, Adrian hesitated as well, then mounted the step and fumbled and then grabbed the ring, giving a sharp rap against the wood. 'Very good.'

'Lord Folbroke?' The butler's greeting was unsure, for it had been a long time since he'd visited. And if the servants' gossip here was as effective as it was in his own home, the whole household must be buzzing since the return of his wife and her brother.

Adrian gave a nod of affirmation and held out his hat, hoping that the man could understand the nature of his difficulty by the vagueness of his gaze. 'And an associate,' he said, gesturing down to the boy with his other hand. 'Could someone take this young man to the kitchen and feed him? And give him the shilling I have promised him.' He glanced down in the general direction of the child and heard another sniff. 'And wipe his nose.'

Then he reached out, and found the boy's shoulder, giving it a pat. 'And you, lad. If you are interested in honest work, some might be found for you in my house.' If he meant to walk the city in future, a guide would not go amiss. And he suspected a child of the streets should know them better than most.

'Yes, sir,' the boy answered.

'Yes, my lord,' Adrian corrected. 'Now get some dinner into yourself and wait until I can figure what is to be done with you.'

Then he turned back, looking down the entrance hall of his brother-in-law's home and trying to remember what he could of the arrangement. The butler stood behind him, still awaiting an explanation. 'Is my wife in residence?' he asked. 'I wish to speak with her.'

He suspected the man had nodded, for there was no immediate answer, so he tipped his head and prompted, 'I am sorry, I could not hear that.'

The man cleared his throat. 'Yes, my lord. If you would wait in the salon...'

Adrian felt the touch on his arm, and shrugged it away. 'If you would describe the way to me, I prefer to walk under my own power.' The man gave him instructions, and Adrian reached out with his stick to tap the way into the sitting room.

As he crossed the threshold, he heard a gasp from the left, on the other side of the hall. Higher than it should be. There were stairs, certainly. And a woman in soft slippers, running down them with short light steps.

'Adrian.' Her voice was breathless and girlish, as he had remembered it, as though she could not quite overcome the awe she felt, and her pace was that of his eager young bride.

But now, before she reached him, she slowed herself

so he would not think her too tractable, and changed her tone. 'Adrian.' In a few paces she had changed from the girl he'd left to the woman who had come to London for him. She was still angry with him. And pretending to be quite unimpressed with his arrival.

'You notice I have come to you.' He held his arms wide for her, hoping that she would step into them.

'It is about time,' she said. 'According to David, you never visit him here any more, though it is not far, and the way is not unknown to your coachman. Not an onerous journey at all. Hardly worthy of comment.'

He stepped a little closer to inhale her scent. *Lemons*. His mouth watered for her. 'I did not request a coach. The night is clear, the breeze fresh. And so I walked.'

He thought he heard a faint gasp of surprise.

'I very nearly got lost along the way. But there was a boy in the street, trying to pick my pocket. And so I caught him, and forced him to help me.'

Now he could imagine the little quirk of her mouth, as though she said the next stern words through half a smile. 'That was very resourceful of you. There is no shame, you know, admitting that you need help from time to time. Nor should a minor setback on the journey keep you from taking it.'

'Trying to teach me independence, are you?'

'I think you do not need teaching in that. It is dependence that you fear.'

'True enough.' It had made him resist her for far too long. 'It was wrong of you to lie to me, you know. I felt quite foolish, to think I had been seducing my own wife.'

And now he had wrong footed it, for that sounded like she was not worth the effort.

The smile was gone from her voice. 'If you had not kept the truth from me in the first place, then I would not have needed to lie to you. And I doubt you'd have bothered to seduce me at all, had you known who I was. If the first week of our marriage was any indication of our future, you'd have grown bored and left me by now.' Her voice was smaller, and with the breathless lack of confidence that he remembered from the girl he had married. Then there was the tiniest sniff, as though she might have a tear in her eye at the thought, but it was stifled and replaced with the firmer resolve of the new Emily. 'And I would have found a less tame lover to satisfy me.'

Damn the woman. He had forgotten her assessment of his abilities, in the early days of their union. And she had chosen to remind him of it, in a common hallway where anyone might hear. He stepped the rest of the way into the salon and pulled her in after him, closing the door so that they could be alone together. Then he let the heat of anger spread lower in him, to change to another kind of heat entirely. 'Or you would have learned to speak aloud what you wished from me, so that you were sure I understood. I am blind, you know, and need an understanding woman.' He tried to sound pitiful.

But she was having none of it. 'Your eyes were good enough when we married, and yet you were blind to my charms.'

'Which are considerable,' he added. 'Given a little

time, I'd have discovered them. It is far more likely that I would have crept away to London by now just to get some rest.' He leaned closer to her, so that he could whisper into her ear, 'I swear, after only a week in your company, I am exhausted by your appetites.'

'Exhausted already?' She was definitely smiling again. 'I thought it was just getting interesting. But, of course, you had already begun to think of another while you bedded me. Some paragon of innocence and common sense named Emily who is most unlike me.' She caught him by the lapel and fumbled in his coat pocket to be sure that the locket was still where he always carried it. 'And she is most unattractive, to judge by this likeness.'

He gripped her wrist to stay her hand. 'She is a goddess.'

'Your picture of her is spoiled.'

'And yet I am loathe to part with it. It got me through Talavera unscathed, and many other battles after that one. I do not need to see it, for I carried it halfway across Portugal and I memorised every line.'

'Really.' There was a quiet awe in her voice as she softened to him, and he knew he had won. 'But I am not the girl in the picture any more. I have changed, Adrian.'

He eased the locket from her hand, and replaced it in his pocket, marvelling that he had not known her from the first. 'Not as much as you think. You were beautiful then, and you are beautiful now. Emily,' he said, enjoying the sound of the word on his lips and the little cooing noise she made when he named her. 'Emily.' His body tightened in anticipation, just knowing she was with him after so long. 'Have I ever told you how completely I love you?'

'I don't believe you have.' She leaned against him until his shoulders bumped against the door behind them.

'I expect you will hear it frequently, now that I have returned to you.' He kissed her gently, marvelling at how right it felt, holding her close, enjoying the warmth of her body, the now familiar curves of it, and the smell of her hair, and wondering why he had been foolish enough to deny himself.

And then he remembered what she had said to him on the night that they had spoken of their marriages. 'Three times?'

'I beg your pardon?'

'You told me that your husband had made love to you only three times, before leaving you.'

'Yes, Adrian,' she said, giving an impatient little stamp of her foot. 'Of course, the number is greater after this week. Now it is four. Or perhaps four and a half. I am not sure how to count some of the things that have happened.'

'But still. Three times.' He shook his head in amazement. 'I could swear it was more.'

'And you would be wrong. It was only three.' She pressed her body tight to his. 'Now you are treating me so politely that it makes me wonder if I must force you to tend to your obligations.'

'My obligations?' he asked.

'To your wife,' she said significantly. And she slipped

her hands beneath his vest, spreading her fingers over his ribs, then tugging at the tails of his shirt. She was eager for him again. And he remembered what Hendricks had said, and did his best not to wonder at the reason for it.

He stayed her hands. 'Before we continue. When I went to White's yesterday, I chanced to meet Rupert.'

'How unfortunate for you,' she responded. 'But it explains the nonsense you were ranting at me a few hours ago. Your cousin has been harassing me endlessly in Derbyshire over your absence. You had been away so long that he had begun to doubt your existence.' She went up on her toes to kiss him, catching his lower lip in her teeth and nibbling upon it.

'Rupert is a blockhead,' he muttered around the kiss, wondering if he cared one way or the other for the truth. If she meant to distract him from it, she was doing a damn fine job, for her hands had started to move again, reaching for the buttons of his trousers. 'The next time he visits, I will box his ears and send him on his way. As I wished I could have yesterday. He was quick to offer me congratulations on the impending birth. I assured him that you told the truth, of course. And that I was very happy. As I am, of course.' He felt her shoulders begin to shake and feared that tears were imminent. He reached up to wipe them from her cheek and his hand felt nothing but her soft, kissable skin. 'What the devil? You are laughing at me. What do you find so amusing about this?'

'That you insist on being so noble about my poor unwanted child.' Her hands left his body, and he heard the rustle of her skirts and felt the hems brushing his fingers as she drew them up to her waist, then pressed his hands against her belly to prove to him that it was soft, flat and empty. 'Have you not touched me here often enough to find the truth?'

'I was not paying attention,' he said. Nor was he now. He was too busy feeling the bottom of her stays, the tops of her stockings, and all the delicious flesh in between. He ran a finger under the bow in her garter. 'This is new.'

A silk-clad leg twined about his to help her balance as she kissed his throat. 'Your darling Emily is a virtuous lady and does not go naked beneath her gown. But there are limits to my propriety. Your tiresome cousin would not stop bothering me about his plans for the estate when he was Folbroke. So to put him off, I told him I was pregnant with your child and he had been cut out of the succession.'

'You little liar. Do you know what agonies I went through, thinking you loved another?'

'I suspect I do. For I have felt them every day that we have been parted.'

He winced, imagining the pain of the last day, magnified by weeks and months and years, and then pulled her close to him for a kiss that was not nearly enough to expiate it. But it seemed to help, for she purred in satisfaction against the skin of his throat. 'Tell me, when you discovered this supposed truth about my infidelity, did you rush your mistress's bed so that you might vent your frustrations?'

'Perhaps,' he admitted.

'Then I hope that we might go back to my rooms to be alone, and that you are similarly frustrated tonight.'

He remembered their lovemaking of the previous night, and her eager response to it, after her lies to Rupert. 'And when my cousin came back in nine months with a christening gift, where were you planning to get a baby?'

'From you, of course. I came to London to seduce you.'

They were the last words he had thought to hear from his wife. Not unwelcome, of course. Merely unexpected. In response, his pulse increased and his mind filled with possibilities.

'And do not tell me that you do not want a child, for I will not hear of it. Sighted or blind, it will not matter, as long as he has a strong father to show him the way.'

'You think that, do you?' He could not help smiling at the prospect. For a child who had such a mother could not help but grow right.

'And his brothers and sisters as well.'

'Brothers and sisters?'

'You do not know it,' she assured him, 'but brothers, when they are not cutting up one's peace, are a great comfort.'

'We do not have one, yet, and you are already planning a family.'

'And I am quite tired of planning,' she whispered. 'Now that you have taught me what it means to act on the desire.'

He gave a weary sigh, as though it was a burden to

please her and to hide how perfectly wicked he found her plan, now that he had grown used to it. 'You are a most trying woman, my Lady Folbroke. If that is all that will please you, then I am tired of fighting you on it. Take me, and get it over with.'

'As you wish, my lord.' And she was reaching for his buttons again. He grabbed for her wrists. He had not expected that she would take him seriously and now things were getting quite out of hand.

'Emily.' That had been a mistake. For while the feeling of her hands was making him hard, speaking that beloved name nearly made him lose control. 'Can you not wait until I might take you to bed?'

She tugged at the end of his cravat with her teeth. 'I have waited three years, Adrian.' She pulled her hands up until she could kiss his fingers, sucking the tips of them into her mouth. He released her hands, trying not to imagine the lurid things that he wished to do with the mother of those future children.

He would act on them, in time. Soon, he reminded himself, firmly. Very soon. Just not now. He had a lifetime with her. Surely he could wait a few minutes, until they could go to her rooms. Or his. He withdrew his fingers and ran them over her face, tracing her smile, her cheeks, her jaw, in a chaste examination of each feature. How could he not have known this face? It should have been as familiar to him as his own. 'You are so lovely,' he said, trying to fill the void of neglect he had created with a more worthy emotion than lust. 'If you mean to take the locket from me, then I must find something else to carry, so that I can share your beauty with others while I enjoy it myself. Will you sit for a cameo?'

She stepped with her little slipper-covered feet onto his boots to make it easier to kiss him. 'What a clever idea.'

'It is, isn't it?' He smiled and ran a finger down her cheek. 'Something Greek, I think. I see you posed as Athena.'

'Aphrodite,' she offered, 'with bare shoulders.'

He ran his fingers lower, touching her throat. 'And bare there as well. And here.' His fingers touched her skirt, still raised and crushed between them, and remembered the treasures exposed beneath it. 'Perhaps an artfully arranged drape,' he conceded, stroking diagonally across her body until his hand rested on her bare hip.

'And you could touch me, whenever you liked,' she encouraged. And her hands slipped lower again.

'This is madness,' he said, without much conviction. 'Stop it this instant.'

'Why?' she whispered.

'Because we are in a salon and not a bedroom. It is not respectful of your brother. It is not proper.' He tried to think of other reasons. But as she exposed him, stroked him and eased him between her legs, he did nothing to stop her.

'And I am your wife and not your lover,' she said, stopping herself. In her voice, he heard the hesitance and resignation that had been there on their first nights together.

She was soft, warm and willing. And he was harder

than he'd ever been for her. The contact with her body made every nerve in him tingle with eagerness. The air was full of the scent of lemons, and he was wasting time with propriety. 'You are both,' he said. 'Wife and lover. Let me prove it to you.' Then he leaned back against the door, shifted his weight, bent his knees, found her body and lost himself.

The next minutes were a blur. His hand behind her knee. Her leg wrapped around his hip. His hand on her breast. Her mouth on his, kissing as though she could suck the life from him. And their bodies meeting, over and over in subtle, silent thrusts so as not to summon the servants or alert his childhood friend to the delightful debauchery taking place in his home. And all the while, the thought echoing in his head was that most men would give two good eyes for the opportunity to have a woman like this, even for a single night.

But the lascivious creature panting out her climax in his ear was his wife. His Emily. Emily. Emily. And he finished in her with a soul-wrenching shudder, and a single rattle of the door that they rested against. As their bodies calmed, he held her, amazed.

Behind them, the door rattled, and bounced against his shoulders as though someone was attempting to open it. 'What the devil?'

'David,' Adrian said, remembering why he had resisted this interlude. 'A moment, please.'

'Folbroke?' There was a moment of suspicious silence. 'And I suppose my sister is in there with you.'

He smiled, and said, 'My wife. Yes.'

'We are working out our differences,' Emily said, with the smallest sway of her hips before she parted from him and let her skirts fall back into place with a rustle.

'But must you do it in the salon?' David muttered from the hall.

His wife was giggling into his lapel and smoothing his clothing back into place as he said, 'My apologies for the momentary lapse of judgement, Eston. It was…' he rolled his eyes towards heaven for the benefit of Emily '…unavoidable. In a moment, we will be retiring to Emily's rooms, and will bother you no further.'

'But perhaps you might join us for dinner,' Emily offered.

'Later in the week,' Adrian added.

'Several days from now,' she corrected.

From the other side of the door, there was a disgusted snort and the sound of retreating footsteps. Emily burst into another fit of giggling, then she was reaching for him again.

This time he stopped her, ignoring her pouts and the demands of his own body. 'Lady Folbroke, your behaviour is disgraceful.' And then he whispered in her ear, 'And I was a fool to have run from you.'

'Yes, you were,' she agreed. 'But you are my fool, and you will not get away from me again.'

'Quite true.' He grinned. 'Thanks to you, I think I will be the first in a long line of Folbrokes to die in his bed.'

* * * * *

HISTORICAL

Where Love is Timeless™

HARLEQUIN® HISTORICAL

COMING NEXT MONTH
AVAILABLE MARCH 27, 2012

A COWBOY WORTH CLAIMING
The Worths of Red Ridge
Charlene Sands
(Western)

MARRIED TO A STRANGER
Danger & Desire
Louise Allen
(Regency)

LADY DRUSILLA'S ROAD TO RUIN
Ladies in Disgrace
Christine Merrill
Three delectably disgraceful ladies,
breaking every one of society's rules,
each in need of a rake to tame them!
(Regency)

**TALL, DARK AND
DISREPUTABLE**
Deb Marlowe
(Regency)

REQUEST YOUR FREE BOOKS!

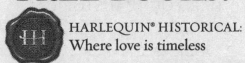

HARLEQUIN® HISTORICAL:
Where love is timeless

2 FREE NOVELS PLUS 2 **FREE GIFTS!**

YES! Please send me 2 FREE Harlequin® Historical novels and my 2 FREE gifts (gifts are worth about $10). After receiving them, if I don't wish to receive any more books, I can return the shipping statement marked "cancel." If I don't cancel, I will receive 6 brand-new novels every month and be billed just $5.19 per book in the U.S. or $5.74 per book in Canada. That's a savings of at least 17% off the cover price! It's quite a bargain! Shipping and handling is just 50¢ per book in the U.S. and 75¢ per book in Canada.* I understand that accepting the 2 free books and gifts places me under no obligation to buy anything. I can always return a shipment and cancel at any time. Even if I never buy another book, the two free books and gifts are mine to keep forever.

246/349 HDN FEQQ

Name _____ (PLEASE PRINT)

Address _____ Apt. #

City _____ State/Prov. _____ Zip/Postal Code

Signature (if under 18, a parent or guardian must sign)

Mail to the **Reader Service:**
IN U.S.A.: P.O. Box 1867, Buffalo, NY 14240-1867
IN CANADA: P.O. Box 609, Fort Erie, Ontario L2A 5X3

Not valid for current subscribers to Harlequin Historical books.

Want to try two free books from another line?
Call 1-800-873-8635 or visit www.ReaderService.com.

* Terms and prices subject to change without notice. Prices do not include applicable taxes. Sales tax applicable in N.Y. Canadian residents will be charged applicable taxes. Offer not valid in Quebec. This offer is limited to one order per household. All orders subject to credit approval. Credit or debit balances in a customer's account(s) may be offset by any other outstanding balance owed by or to the customer. Please allow 4 to 6 weeks for delivery. Offer available while quantities last.

Your Privacy—The Reader Service is committed to protecting your privacy. Our Privacy Policy is available online at www.ReaderService.com or upon request from the Reader Service.

We make a portion of our mailing list available to reputable third parties that offer products we believe may interest you. If you prefer that we not exchange your name with third parties, or if you wish to clarify or modify your communication preferences, please visit us at www.ReaderService.com/consumerschoice or write to us at Reader Service Preference Service, P.O. Box 9062, Buffalo, NY 14269. Include your complete name and address.

HHIIB

*Taft Bowman knew he'd ruined any chance he'd had
for happiness with Laura Pendleton when he drove her
away years ago...and into the arms of another man,
thousands of miles away. Now she was back, a widow
with two small children...and despite himself, he was
starting to believe in second chances.*

Harlequin Special® Edition® presents a new installment
in USA TODAY bestselling author
RaeAnne Thayne's miniseries,
THE COWBOYS OF COLD CREEK.

*Enjoy a sneak peek of
A COLD CREEK REUNION*

Available April 2012 from Harlequin® Special Edition®

A younger woman stood there, and from this distance he
had only a strange impression, as though she was somehow standing on an island of calm amid the chaos of the
scene, the flashing lights of the emergency vehicles, shouts
between his crew members, the excited buzz of the crowd.

And then the woman turned and he just about tripped
over a snaking fire hose somebody shouldn't have left
there.

Laura.

He froze, and for the first time in fifteen years as a fire-
fighter, he forgot about the incident, his mission, just what
the hell he was doing here.

Laura.

Ten years. He hadn't seen her in all that time, since
the week before their wedding when she had given him
back his ring and left town. Not just town. She had left the
whole damn country, as if she couldn't run far enough to

get away from him.

Some part of him desperately wanted to think he had made some kind of mistake. It couldn't be her. That was just some other slender woman with a long sweep of honey-blond hair and big, blue, unforgettable eyes. But no. It was definitely Laura. Sweet and lovely.

Not his.

He was going to have to go over there and talk to her. He didn't want to. He wanted to stand there and pretend he hadn't seen her. But he was the fire chief. He couldn't hide out just because he had a painful history with the daughter of the property owner.

Sometimes he hated his job.

Will Taft and Laura be able to make the years recede...or is the gulf between them too broad to ever cross?

Find out in
A COLD CREEK REUNION
Available April 2012 from Harlequin® Special Edition®
wherever books are sold.

Celebrate the 30th anniversary
of Harlequin® Special Edition® with a bonus story
included in each Special Edition® book in April!

HSEEXP0412

LOVE INSPIRED HISTORICAL

HEART-WARMING ROMANCES THAT SPEAK OF HOPE, LOVE AND THE FUTURE!

celebrating **15** YEARS

A collection of three Western novellas in which unexpected reunions lead to second chances at love...and delightful spring weddings!

Brides of the West

Josie's Wedding Dress	by Victoria Bylin
Last Minute Bride	by Janet Dean
Her Ideal Husband	by Pamela Nissen

Available April wherever books are sold.

www.LoveInspiredBooks.com

LIH82912